The
Time-Travel
Trail Bride

by

Elizabeth Barstone

Copyright © 2023 Elizabeth Barstone
All Rights Reserved
Paperback Edition
5.25 in x 8 in

ISBN: 978-1-988742-88-5

No part of this book may be reproduced or transmitted in any form or by any means, including but not limited to: graphic, electronic, or mechanical, including photo copying, recording, taping, or by any information storage retrieval system, without the permission, in writing, of the publisher. Infringement of this can and will result in legal action.

This book is a complete work of fiction. No characters, situations, or events are based on real events, situations, or people, living or dead. The entirety of this story is a complete product of the author's imagination.

HSP

Published by Haven Street Publishing
www.havenstreetpublishing.com

The Time-Travel Trail Bride

Contents

Dedicated to all the wild imaginations everywhere!

Chapter 1

"Is something wrong, *Miss* Cooper?" Arwin Beckett asked sarcastically, causing everyone around the long mahogany conference table to stare at me. I immediately stopped tapping my pen. Having a boss that was six years my junior apparently created in him a need to constantly remind me that he was, in fact, my boss.

It's Mrs. Cooper, I habitually corrected him in my mind, but I only said, "No, Mr. Beckett. I was just thinking."

"Well, I've got *two* minutes to spare, what fantastical things were you thinking?" he asked, looking around the table for approval of his insinuation that I was stupid. The men smiled but knew better than to laugh. Not only was Beckett a bigot, but he'd snidely insulted me on numerous occasions, and didn't seem to care if I overheard his insulting blonde jokes or not. *I,* on the other hand, was extremely careful not to let him hear me refer to him as Arwin Bigot behind his back.

"Well?" Arwin said. "If you're going to think on company time, especially *my* time, you better have a winning proposal up there!" He gave a weak little forced laugh, apparently trying to encourage my coworkers to laugh along with him. Everyone just stared blankly at him and waited for me to speak.

I was *not* going to tell him I'd been thinking

about how absent my husband had been lately. How I'd been trying to determine one way or the other if he was cheating on me or if I was just paranoid because he'd had to work late so many nights. Instead, I forced my eyes to focus on the document before me.

"I was just thinking about the Carpenter account," I lied. "If we outsource a couple of people, we can bring the project in under budget and a week early."

"How?" Beckett asked, scrunching up his thin lips and obviously expecting me to fail. He shot a snide glance at Frank sitting beside him. I had as little respect for Frank as I had for Beckett, but I couldn't allow my personal feelings to interfere with the promotion that I was definitely due.

"Outsourcing the small parts of the project will allow us to focus on the more complicated aspects, and without all the small distractions, we'll get done quicker," I said. Of course it made common sense. I didn't tell him I'd been doing this all along anyway even without his permission because of the unreasonable amount of work he piled on me. I was a problem solver, and that was why I was the preferred marketing manager of all clients with the company.

In fact, I would be surprised if I didn't get the promotion to regional manager when the performance reviews were done next week. Thankfully, those were being done by corporate this year since too many employees had secretly reported Beckett to head office. Rumors had been circulating for weeks that he was going to be fired. This had apparently never reached his own ears, because he was still the same obnoxious tyrant he'd been since the day he was hired. *The day after I was told I was being promoted to the regional manager position!*

"No, we don't have the budget for it," Arwin said in his usual dismissive fashion.

"But it will cost *less,*" I insisted.

"No," Arwin said firmly. "And that's final. I'm not going to take away work from our staff to outsource to a bunch of nobodies."

"I wouldn't be surprised if it's just a bunch of freelancers that's been doing her work anyway," Lucy Hemper said under her breath, with a slight huff. Lucy had never made any attempt to pretend to like me. Despite working six years together at the same advertising agency, Lucy still treated me like an invader. I was wise enough to see through the thin shield of jealousy and did my best to ignore her. But now with major promotions coming up, everyone was at each other's throats. Even those that had displayed some semblance of friendship.

I felt my face turn red when my phone rang in my bag.

"I said no phones during meetings, Taylor," Beckett said slowly, glaring at me. "If you need to leave to go take care of your kids, just go."

"It could be a client," I shot back. I yanked the phone out of my bag and hoped that it was a client, or at least someone I could fake as a client. But it was Amber, my 12-year-old. "It *is* a client, and I *have* to take this," I lied, standing to leave the room.

"Go on, you won't be missed," Beckett said, waving his hand as though he were dismissing a servant. "Hey, Taylor! While you're out there, do you wanna bring me a coffee?"

I pretended I hadn't heard and hurried from the

conference room as I answered the call.

"Amber, what is it?" I asked, unable to hide the annoyance in my voice.

"Dad still isn't home," Amber said into the phone. "The daycare called and said you need to pick up Emily."

"What?" I shrieked. "Okay, thanks for letting me know. I gotta go."

"We ordered pizza for supper," Amber said hurriedly. "We saved you some!"

I let out a sigh. "Okay," I said. "I'll be home soon." *Cold pizza.* I had purposely prepared a casserole the night before and told Neil to just heat it up when he got home. *Why wasn't he home already?* My usual worry kicked in, and I envisioned him in a car crash, bloody and near death, or worse.

I called Neil, and my worry turned to anger as soon as I heard his voice.

"I thought you were picking up Emily today," I said.

"Oh crap!" he exclaimed. I heard a rustle that sounded exactly the way he threw the sheet off him every morning. I'd been listening to it for 12 years; I *knew* what I heard. "What time is it?" I could hear the rustling of his clothing.

"It's almost six," I told him. "I *told* you I had a late meeting today. You were supposed to pick her up a half-hour ago."

"Dammit," Neil said.

"Where *are* you?" I demanded. "Did you go home and go to bed or something?"

"I'm leaving work," he said. I heard him blow

air out.

"Are you *smoking* again?" I asked.

"No, no," he said, but I knew he was lying. I'd put up with him smoking for years before he gave it up.

"So, are you going to get Emily?" I asked, debating whether returning to the meeting was even worth it at this point.

"It's gonna take me about twenty minutes to get there," Neil said. "You better get her."

"I'm in a meeting!" I reminded him. "Where *are* you that you're twenty minutes away from her daycare? You work downtown! You're as close as I am!"

"You'll have to get her!" Neil said angrily. "I'll be home in a half-hour!"

He hung up. Apparently, Neil *also* thought I was stupid. *It must be a man thing,* I thought. *Do all men think all women are stupid?* I wondered.

I tried to push thoughts of Neil cheating on me *again* out of my head. As far as I knew, the last time had been the *last* time. And that was four years ago. I could hear my mother's voice in my head, *A leopard doesn't change his spots!* I wished I'd listened to my mother back when I'd first met Neil. She'd warned me about him, but I'd been young and in love. I admitted that back then, I *had* been stupid. I wished I still had my mother here. What I wouldn't give to tell her I'd been wrong about everything. Every bit of advice she'd ever given me had been right. And I'd been a pigheaded teenager and adult, ignoring her aged wisdom. And now she was gone. She'd died only two weeks after Amber had been born.

"Get some sleep, Taylor!" Beckett shouted behind me as everyone streamed out of the conference room. "Don't just stand there in a daze. And I want those client reports on my desk at 8 a.m.!"

"I don't have them ready!" I said. "I said I'd have them in by Friday!"

"Tomorrow," he said with a slimy grin. "8 a.m.!"

He walked past as everyone else went to their offices to get ready to leave. I just stood there, frozen, and watched them all go, like corporate robots.

I shook my head, trying to physically bring myself back to the present. My therapist had told me numerous times it wasn't good to think about the past all the time. I tried not to, but I couldn't help it when my life had been such a mess; one disaster after another.

Although, I couldn't really call Amber a disaster. An *accident*, yes, but not a disaster. I continued to dwell on my mistakes as I robotically went to my office, shut down my computer, and grabbed my purse and my jacket.

Emily's waiting! The image of my three-year-old cherub with her blonde curls invaded my memories. She had been a marriage-saver baby. That's what Mom would've called her. A baby born with the sole purpose of saving a marriage. It was a lot of responsibility to put on a baby.

My self-anger at my past stupidity followed me into the elevator and to the parking lot. Amber had been the reason I'd married Neil. I was young, twenty, and had wanted to have a happy family like my parents had had. I was naïve enough to think that being pregnant had been a good reason to get married. I was thrilled when she was born. She'd been the most adorable newborn

I'd ever seen, and with her head covered with yellowish tufts of hair, she was given the name Amber.

If I'd known that she would barely know her father anyway because he'd be gone all the time, running around with other women, frequenting bars and night clubs, I would've listened to my mother and never have married him. But it was too late. I couldn't see myself being a divorced woman at twenty-one, so I hung in there, trying to be the best wife and mother that I could be.

Somehow, Neil seemed to mature a little when his friends started getting married and having kids. When his best friend became a father to a chubby little boy, Neil expressed interest in having a son.

I was only twenty-two years old, and my head was still in the clouds. I was thankful that I'd stuck with Neil. He'd stopped hanging out at bars and night clubs, and I could tell he was really trying. When I got pregnant, Neil insisted for the entire pregnancy that he was having a boy. I was so nervous, wondering what he might do if it turned out to be another girl, that I could barely enjoy the prospect of giving little Amber a sibling. It wasn't until an ultrasound confirmed we were having a boy that I relaxed. Neil had stepped up and tried to be the perfect husband. For a while.

At that time, I'd regretted that Mom hadn't lived long enough to see Neil become the husband and father that I'd fantasized about.

Now, at thirty-two, I knew my mother *had* been right all along. Not even a third child had stopped him from cheating.

I pulled into the daycare, cringing at the fact there was only one other car in the parking lot—the administrator's. I hurried in the front door and down the hall where I found my baby sitting on a small bench outside the administrator's office.

"Mommy! You forgot me!" Emily said, her big blue eyes spilling with tears.

"Oh, honey, I'm sorry," I said. "Daddy was supposed to pick you up today!"

"Mrs. Cooper!" A middle-aged woman with thick cat-eye glasses yelled from inside the office. I'd hoped I could escape with my daughter without having to answer to Agnes.

"Hi, Mrs. Lenhorn," I said, picking up Emily, hoping she could function as a shield. I knew Agnes wouldn't yell in front of a child. At least I hoped not. "I'm sorry, Neil was supposed to pick her up."

"This is the *third* time this has happened *this* year," Agnes said with a frown. "And it's only March! We *can't* let this happen again. You will receive a bill for overtime today, and if this happens *one* more time, Emily will be removed from enrollment. Is that clear?"

"Yes," I said with a nod. "I promise."

I turned and left before she could say anything else.

"Am I in trouble?" Emily asked.

"Oh no, sweetie," I told her. "Daddy is in trouble."

"Why is Daddy in trouble?" she asked.

"Never mind," I told her. "Let's go home and have some dinner, okay?"

"I'm hungry!" Emily said. "Mrs. Lenhorn gave me cookies!"

"I'm so sorry that you had to wait," I told her.

Guilt flooded me, and I felt like such a horrible parent. A horrible *person*. As I said, my life had been a trail of mistakes and disasters. One poor decision after another.

Chapter 2

Neil still wasn't home by the time we got home. "I'm home!" I called as I walked in the door with Emily. No one answered. *The usual.*

"Go wash your hands for dinner," I told Emily, as soon as I removed her jacket. I went upstairs to check on the others. "Kids, I'm home."

"Okay," Amber called from her room. I heard video game noises from August's room.

I tapped on Amber's door and opened it. She was on her computer.

"I'm home," I told her.

"I heard," she said, typing away on her laptop without even looking at me.

"You shouldn't spend so much time on social media," I said. "How was school?"

"Same old," she said. Her fingers flew over the keys and her eyes never left the screen.

"Seriously, why don't you come downstairs for a while?" I suggested.

"No, I'm talking to my *friends*," Amber said. "Close the door!"

I left and went to August's room. I was too tired to even try with Amber today, and this was her *good mood!*

"I'm home, did you eat?" I asked. The only thing a ten-year-old boy is interested in is food and video games, I'd learned.

"Yeah," he said without even looking at me. "Rats! You made me mess up!"

"Well, why don't you take a break and come downstairs," I said.

"Why?" he asked, restarting his game and not even looking at me. "I'm busy."

"Did you do your homework?" I asked.

"I didn't have any," he said. "Mom! You're making me lose! *Go away!*"

I was too tired to get into an argument about how he shouldn't speak to me. I knew I'd be better off saving my energy for the bed time battle. August had been spoiled by his father for the formative years of his life and now, even at ten years old, he would launch into a full-blown tantrum to get his way, while his father would simply say, "boys will be boys." I hated to admit to myself that sometimes I couldn't stand my own child. Not *him,* but his *behavior!*

My therapist had replaced my mother, but the advice was always more or less the same. Three kids and a cheating husband had put me into therapy, which—while not that helpful in terms of improving my life—gave me an hour each week where someone *had* to sit and listen to what was on my mind without criticizing me.

Amber and August had ordered two large pizzas and had devoured one between them, leaving the second open on the table, where Stanley, our big orange adopted stray had discovered it. Stanley skedaddled as soon as he saw me, and he hadn't had time to actually eat any of it; at least that I could tell. I was hungry enough to blow it off in case of cat hair and pop a large piece into the microwave.

"I don't *like* pizza," Emily said. "I want cereal."

It's one of those days, I decided. A day where it just didn't matter. *Who cares if for one day a preschooler eats cereal for dinner and her mother eats reheated pizza, possibly with cat germs in it?*

"Mommy, are you okay?" Emily asked when I set a bowl of her favorite cereal in front of her. "You *always* make me eat what you cook."

As we sat at the table, eating the poor excuse for a meal, I felt like a complete failure. My older kids were obnoxious, and Neil still wasn't home, and it was way past six. Emily, the only child who seemed to want to talk to me, chattered nonstop about the other kids at day-care. I felt even guiltier when I realized I hadn't even been paying attention.

I need to fix my life! I decided. *I need to do something! I hate my job! I hate the way everything is going! I need to make a change. Somehow.* But the problem was, I didn't know how. How could I change something that had been in motion so long there was no stopping it?

I forced myself to focus on Emily and participate in her conversation, and it was after she was bathed, read to, and tucked in that Neil arrived home.

"Where *were* you?" I demanded as soon as he walked in the door. I hated being the nagging wife, but he was the one that had created that role for me. "It's after seven!"

"I got held up," he said, brushing past me and heading up the stairs. "I need to take a shower."

"Yeah, you do!" I said, following him up the stairs and into the bedroom. "You reek of perfume! Who

18

were you with?" My heart sank. *He was cheating on me*.

"No one!" he said, pulling clean clothes from the dresser. "Quit being so jealous! If you keep being such a nag, you're gonna drive me to cheat!"

I need to make changes! The thought plagued me. I somehow had to *fix* all this. I had to fix my marriage.

"Wait!" I said, pulling on his arm as he left the bedroom, causing him to turn sideways, which pulled the sleeve of his work shirt just enough that it lowered the collar. There in plain sight was a *hickey!* A large red hickey that would've taken some time to create. By the time the words were out of my mouth, I didn't even mean them anymore. "I want us to go to marriage counselling!"

Chapter 3

Neil yanked his arm away from me and headed silently to the shower. I knew what I'd seen, and I knew what it meant. My husband was *definitely* having an affair. I knew what my mother would say. She would tell me that staying in a marriage for the sake of the kids was never a good idea. *Was that my mother's voice in my head, or my therapist's?* Sometimes it was hard to tell. I felt like I was going insane.

The thought of my marriage crumbling was unbearable, and I pushed it out of my head immediately. I couldn't think of divorce. Not right now. Not when I had a dozen client reports to prepare for the morning, and a ten-year-old tantrum to deal with at nine.

I sat at the kitchen table with my laptop and worked on my reports until it was August's bedtime. Then I braced myself for the nightly routine. At least dealing with that was easier than dealing with a divorce.

At nine, I went back upstairs. "It's bedtime," I said firmly.

"But I need to do my homework," August whined.

"Then you shouldn't have been playing your video games," I told him. "Bedtime, now!"

"If I don't do my homework, I'll get in trouble at school!" he said.

"So?" I said. "Then you won't avoid doing your

homework again!" *Not tonight, bucko! You're not going to win this round!*

"You're seriously not gonna let me do my homework?" August stood in the middle of the room with his jaw hanging. I wasn't going to let his pitiful stance influence me.

"Look, Augie," I said. "Your homework is *your* problem, not mine. I did all my homework when I was in school. Do your homework, don't do your homework, I don't care! I'm not the one that has to deal with the teacher at school tomorrow."

My son just stood and stared at me, and I felt a small victory. This was the first time he hadn't manipulated me into staying up an extra hour.

"Well, it's not like my parents are ever home!" he said. "What else was I supposed to do after I ate dinner? You weren't here to tell me to do my homework."

"First of all, you said you didn't have homework when I asked you earlier," I said. "And didn't your teacher *tell* you that you had homework?"

"Yes," he admitted sullenly.

"Then what did you need *me* to tell you for?" I asked. "Get to bed!"

I turned and left, not really caring if he went to bed or not. If he stayed up late, he'd be tired in the morning. Again, that was not my problem at this point. I was fed up.

I went back downstairs and worked on my reports. I was tired, distracted, and plagued by the thought that maybe August thought I didn't care about him. I just felt like putting my head in my hands and crying, but Amber came down to get a snack.

"August isn't in bed," she said.

"I don't care," I said.

"What's wrong with you?" she asked, rummaging through the fridge and finding nothing, headed for the pantry. "Why are you so cranky?"

"Nothing," I said. "Just work."

"Is it too late to ask you to take me to the store?" she asked, pulling out a bag of chips.

"Store? For what?" I asked.

"My science project is due tomorrow, and I ran out of glue," she said.

"Use tape," I said.

"I can't use tape," she said. "I need to use glue."

"Well, look in the junk drawer," I said. "There's probably some wood glue in there."

"I can't use wood glue," she said.

"You waited until the last minute to do your project, and now you expect me to drop what I'm doing and drive you to the store?" I asked in disbelief.

"It's not my fault I ran out of glue," she said, staring at me dumbfounded. "It's just a five-minute drive to the mall."

"Ask your father," I said.

"He's still in the shower."

"Ask him when he's out."

"The mall will be closed by then!"

"Amber, I am tired," I said. "I am exhausted, actually, and stressed about work and a million other things. I need to get these reports done before I go to bed, and I'm not even halfway finished. How many times have I told you not to wait until the last minute to do your projects?"

"So, can you drive me to the mall or not?" she

asked, standing with one hand on her hip.

"No, I cannot," I said.

"Mom, I can't afford to fail," she whined.

"Get your jacket," I said begrudgingly. "But if you *ever* wait until the last minute to tell me you need something for your project, I will *not* be helping you, do you understand?"

"Thanks, Mom!" she said and bounced out of the kitchen.

I grabbed my jacket and purse and headed to the car. It was after ten when we got back home. Amber set off to finish her last-minute project, and I headed back to the kitchen to finish typing up my reports.

I could tell Neil had been in the kitchen by the dirty dishes in the sink and the empty pizza box on the counter. I restrained myself from throwing a fit of my own, as well as the urge to clean the kitchen, and I sat back down to finish my work.

It was well after midnight when I closed my laptop, and I was tired enough that I didn't care that I would be sleeping next to a lying, cheating snake for the night. I welcomed the comfort of my bed and ignored Neil as he snored away, reeking of a mixture of shampoo and alcohol.

After listening to him snore for about fifteen minutes, my exhaustion turned to anger, and I pined for revenge. Not a violent sort of revenge, more like a passive aggressive inconvenient kind of revenge.

I knew he always left his phone charging on his nightstand all night because by bedtime it was drained, and I also knew that he used his phone for his alarm clock in the mornings. I knew by his snoring that even a fire alarm wouldn't disturb his slumber, so I bravely got out of bed and tiptoed around to his side. I unplugged his phone charger from the wall.

I felt such an overwhelming sense of justice by this benign act, that my mind raced to what other things I could do to inconvenience him. I had to credit Stanley for the next act of revenge. When the cat jumped on Neil's dresser, I had an idea.

I hurried to the bathroom where the litter pan was and scooped out some cat crap and deposited it in Neil's underwear drawer. *Hah! Try turning a mistress on with dirty underwear!*

Chapter 4

In the light of day, my childish antics from the night before weren't as funny, and I knew the adult solution would be to file for divorce. Neil overslept, freaked out and swore at the cat when he discovered his underwear drawer, which had been conveniently left open.

I regretted my behavior, but it was too late to undo it. *Well, at least I have something new to discuss with my therapist this week,* I thought.

I was on my way out the door with the kids when Neil came running downstairs. "What the hell happened to my phone?" he shrieked.

"Not my problem," I said. "Listen, you need to pick up Emily today, do you hear me?"

"Yes, yes," he said, running to the kitchen. "Why in the hell didn't you wake me up?"

"I'm not your mother," I shouted. "Do not forget to pick up Emily today!"

"I know! Quit nagging!" he screamed. "You know what that damn cat did? He crapped all over my underwear drawer! Do I have any clean underwear in the dryer?"

"Seeya!" I shouted. "And do *not* forget Emily today!"

"What did Stanley do?" Emily asked as I buckled her into her car seat.

"Who knows?" I said.

"Dad said the cat pooped in his underwear drawer!" August informed us, stifling a giggle.

"Eww!" Amber said.

"That's hilarious!" August said and let out a roar of laughter.

"It's gross!" Amber said. "Mom, we have to get rid of that stinky cat!"

At least August appreciated my humorous revenge. I dropped the older kids at their school, and then took Emily into her daycare.

"Daddy will pick you up today, sweetheart," I told her.

"But what if he forgets me again?" she asked. Worry filled her little face.

"Well, I won't have to work late tonight," I told her. "So, I will double check, okay?"

"Okay, Mommy," Emily said.

I gave her a kiss. "I love you, sweetie," I told her. "You have a good day, okay?"

"Okay, and you have a good day too, Mommy," she said. "And I love you, too!"

As soon as I walked out of the daycare, my heart filled with sadness over what my kids and I would be dealing with in the coming months. I knew I would have to file for divorce. It was clear that Neil wasn't going to be the husband or father we needed and deserved. I was tired of the chaos. I somehow needed to find the strength that I'd had when I was younger. The strength I'd had to defy my mother, who knew best. The strength of will I'd had when I believed I could have any life I chose.

Now somehow, I hadn't chosen any of it, but it

was up to *me* to fix it.

As soon as I arrived at the office, I emailed my boss the reports he wanted. I struggled to focus on work, and finally found myself searching for a good local divorce lawyer. I gave her a quick call and we arranged to meet just after lunch. I would definitely have stuff to talk about with my therapist on Friday after work!

I was on the phone with a potential client when I saw the email from Beckett telling me I had to attend another late meeting today. I *knew* what he was doing. He was trying to prove that my family responsibilities were the reason I was not qualified for a raise.

I was tempted to march right into his office and tell him that I was not going to attend a late meeting on such short notice, but I knew that would be detrimental to my job. Especially since I was going to delay my lunch so I could see a lawyer.

When I hung up with the potential client, I closed my eyes for a second. *What am I doing? Why is my life such a mess?* I wished for time to just think. I just wished I could analyze what I was doing wrong and come up with a solution and the courage to fix my marriage. Friday was still a few days away, and I desperately needed someone to talk to.

"Taylor!" I snapped out of it at the sound of Lucy's grating voice. "I said I need the Marsden file!"

"Why? That's *my* client," I told her.

"Arwin wants me to write the press release," she said.

"But I've already started it," I said. "It's *my* client!"

"I'll tell him you won't give it to me!" she said

and turned away.

I didn't have what it takes to deal with both Lucy *and* Arwin Beckett at the same time today. It was almost time for my appointment, so I grabbed my purse and jacket and left my office.

"Taylor!" Beckett called to me as I headed towards the elevator. "I want Lucy to do the press release. She's better at it. You said you wanted to outsource, outsource it to her."

"When I get back from lunch," I said. I didn't care anymore. Lucy could do *all* my work for all I cared at that moment. I needed a break.

As I left the building, I was engulfed in a feeling of never wanting to go back. I just wanted to quit my job. The thought of my impending divorce told me quitting was not possible. *I suppose if I stayed with Neil, the house would be paid for in three years, and then our expenses would be lower. If I quit my job, he would have to stop wasting money.*

The sudden consolation of what my expenses would be if I *didn't* go through with a divorce made me feel a little better. And thus, staying trapped in a bad situation was indeed easier than changing it. *And that,* I realized, *was how I had ruined my life.* I was just too lazy to go through the hard stuff to get to the good stuff. *But what if there wasn't any good stuff?*

The fresh spring air soothed my spirits, and combined with an expensive cup of coffee, gave me the courage to head to the lawyer's office. I told her what I wanted and why, and when she asked about custody, I said I'd be willing to share joint custody, if that's what Neil wanted. I just wanted it over with as soon as possible. She wrote everything down and said she'd draw something up, and I returned to work with a detached feeling of change.

I found that not getting so attached to my work alleviated some of the stress. I felt a surprising sense of relief by offloading some of my work onto Lucy. The timing was perfect. She was trying to prove to the world she worked harder than I did, and I needed time to end my marriage.

My therapist agreed with me on Friday that I was doing the right thing by ending the bad marriage but was surprised that I wavered on a semi-willingness to ignore my husband's indiscretions, at least for a little while longer.

I admitted to her that the call from the lawyer to sign the divorce papers she'd drawn up had freaked me out a little bit. I'd wanted a divorce as fast as possible, but I didn't expect I'd have anything to sign *that* fast. The lawyer said this was what would go before the judge eventually. A copy would be sent to Neil for him to sign or contest, and he'd have a period of time to contest it, and if he did *not* contest it, then it was a simple process of paperwork filing. *Who knew divorce could be that easy? Expensive—but easy.*

By Saturday, I was on pins and needles, knowing that sometime next week, Neil would receive the divorce papers, and I'd have an adult-sized tantrum to deal with.

All morning Neil sat on the couch with August and played video games with him. It was good to see him with his son. I did wish that he would pay as much attention to the girls, but he barely acknowledged them. At least having Neil around was good for August. I tried to make it up to the girls by spending as much time with them as I could on weekends.

While Neil and August battled in video games, I hauled the girls into the kitchen to help me make cookies.

"I *hate* cooking," Amber whined. "I don't see why I can't go to the mall with my friends."

"If that's what you really want, go," I said. I was tired of fighting with people to be with me.

"Do you *really* think you should be making *cookies?*" Neil asked when he and August came into the kitchen for some snacks.

"What do you mean?" I asked as I placed them carefully on a cookie sheet.

"Well, you're getting a little hippy," he said.

"*Hippy?*" I asked. "What do you mean by that?"

"You're gaining weight," he said. "You should lay off the cookies maybe."

I just stared at him and closed my mouth when I was aware it was still hanging open. *The nerve of him!*

"You *do* know I've been paying for a gym membership for both of us, right?" he said. "I'll babysit the kids if you want to go to the gym this afternoon. Work some of that fat off ya."

"I'll go right now," I said. "You can finish the cookies with Emily."

"Okay," he said, scooping up some raw cookie dough and shoving it into his mouth. "It's not like I need to watch *my* weight."

At least he'll be spending time with one of his other kids, I thought. *But that's the last straw!* I was tired of Neil's snide remarks and outright insults.

I ran upstairs and changed into jeans and a T-shirt.

I'd go out alright, but I wasn't going to the gym. I was going to just go out and spend the day by myself. I would finally have my thinking time!

When I came back downstairs and grabbed my jacket and purse to leave, August had joined Neil and Emily in the kitchen and the three of them were having great fun rolling out cookie dough. Perhaps Neil was trying to prove to me that he was a good father. He probably knew he was on thin ice and I'd been thinking about divorce all week. He knew me so well that just showing a little bit of interest in the kids would be enough to think that I'd been wrong and overreacted. Throwing in a jab about how unattractive I was to him was just to put a thought in my mind that I should be lucky to have him. *No one else would want me.* I'd been analyzing him with my therapist for years now. I could read him like a book. He had no idea that I could see what he was doing, but I was *done* giving him a chance to smarten up.

Chapter 5

After driving around town and over-analyzing the past twelve years of my life, I realized that I *deserved* Neil. He hadn't even *pretended* to be family oriented when I'd met him. He'd had an edge about him that had appealed to my naïve middle-class upbringing in a beige house with beige walls, bedding, draperies and carpets. Even our family sedan had been beige. Neil had been anything but beige. He was a disrupter. He still was.

I tried desperately to sort out my inner turmoil and wondered if it was possible to get my therapist to see me *two* days a week instead of one. I was clearly a basket case, and I was torn between wanting to run away from home and resuming my attempts at molding Neil into the perfect husband and father. I realized that neither was a possibility, but I fantasized for just a moment of a perfect life. Of course, in my perfect fantasy, Neil wouldn't be the man I'd marry. I wouldn't erase my kids. Just Neil. I would still have my beautiful children, however obnoxious they might be at times, but I would've chosen better for their father.

I would've gone with my mother's choice of Devin Baxter. He was as beige as you could get. He'd gone to our church, and since I'd known him from childhood, he held little excitement or appeal to me. He was classic boring. A 1950s haircut, all but a tie with his plain white button-up shirt he wore to school and church, and his classic tan dress pants. He was nice, but lacked any kind of personality that caught my attention. Despite the fact that he'd lived across the street all during my child-hood and teenage years, we'd barely spoken outside of our parents' barbecues.

Still, Devin would've been a wise choice, which was exactly what my mother had said when Neil had moved to town. I'd pursued Neil like crazy until I caught him. Now, I would give anything for a chance to even have a conversation with Devin. For all of his lack of personality or charisma, he was smart and kind. The few conversations we had as teenagers were about possibili-ties for the future, both in science and our personal lives. He was a great conversationalist. He had thoughts. In-telligent thoughts. If he'd been a little more dynamic, I would've enjoyed his company more.

Hours went by as I sat in my car, roaming through fields of mental despair, as shoppers went to and from the massive mall, passing by my car and looking as though they had perfectly happy families.

I allowed myself to walk through the various sce-narios of my possible choices. If I spoke to my lawyer and cancelled my divorce, Neil would never change. I knew I couldn't cancel it, despite toying with the thought. Neil would obviously keep the house. I would have to find a new place to live with my three children. I would have to single-handedly support them because Neil would try to get away with as little child support as possible. Still, if we got a cheap apartment, I could probably swing it. The kids wouldn't be happy, but then again, when were they ever?

I jumped at the tapping on my car window.

"Uncle Charlie!" I exclaimed in surprise as I lowered my window. "Hey, what's up?"

"Taylor! You didn't come by to see my invention last weekend," my uncle reminded me. Uncle Charlie was a bit of an armchair scientist and mad professor.

"I'm sorry," I said. "I totally forgot. Things have been so hectic lately."

"That's okay, come on over now if you're not too busy," he invited.

"Um, okay, maybe later," I said vaguely. I was really not in any mood to visit anyone.

"Are you okay?" he asked. "Is it that scoundrel of a husband of yours? Did he leave you?"

"No," I said in surprise. "Why? Why would you think that."

"Nothing," he said. "I just, well, you know, he's a jerk."

"He's home babysitting the kids," I said. "I'm supposed to be at the gym because according to him, I'm getting a little hippy."

"Oh, nonsense!" Uncle Charlie said. "Come on over for lunch! I'll show you my latest inventions! You can head over now, you know where the key is, just let yourself in, and I'll be home in a few minutes as soon as I pick up some parts."

"Okay," I said. That brief conversation with another human being, who wasn't demanding something from me or criticizing me, made me feel a little better. *I really need to be more social,* I thought. Isolation was probably my main problem, I reasoned. I lived inside my head too much!

With my slightly improved mood, I decided to buy a pie for my lunch with Uncle Charlie. Pumpkin pie was his favorite, and whenever I visited, it had become almost expected of me. With both of my parents gone, Uncle Charlie was my only living relative, other than my kids, and he helped fill the gap when my mom had died.

I took my time shopping to allow him enough time to get home. Uncle Charlie owned a junkheap of a car which he'd built himself and somehow had gotten it approved to drive on the road, but in the summer, he preferred his adult-sized tricycle, which he referred to as his three-wheel bike, for short jaunts in town. He was eccentric to say the least.

An hour later, I drove to his house on the edge of town. It was hard to tell if he was home or not, even though his car was parked in his dusty driveway. Even if he'd been driving his bike, he kept it in his garage when he was home.

I parked behind his rusty vehicle and noticed how it was filled with random steel car parts, radio parts, and wires. He was always building something.

He must've taken his car, I thought. *He'd said he was buying parts.*

I knocked on the door and tried the knob. It was unlocked. *So, he did make it home before me.*

"Uncle Charlie!" I called from the door. "I'm here!"

I knew I was welcome any time in his home, so I took the liberty to explore the living room and kitchen, but he was nowhere in sight. I set the pie and groceries on the counter and called up the stairs. I noticed the basement door was open. *He must've gone right down to his workshop,* I decided and started down the wooden steps to what he referred to as his lab.

The light was on in the basement, confirming my thoughts. "Uncle Charlie," I called. "I'm here!"

No answer.

I looked around. It had been a few months since I'd been by to see his inventions. He had various machines on multiple tabletops, with drawings scattered everywhere, some had fallen to the floor. I couldn't make any sense of the diagrams.

"Uncle Charlie, are you home?" I called, continuing to look around.

I walked through another door and into a little room which had always been cluttered with junk and car parts. Now, it was completely bare except for a podium in the center of the room. *Maybe he's been practicing for his Nobel Prize speech again,* I thought.

Curiosity got the better of me, and I had to know if there was a written speech on his podium. *If it's a public speech, it's not private,* I reasoned. Besides, he'd always made me listen to his various renditions of it before.

I stepped up to the podium, but instead of a speech on it, he'd wired it with a bunch of buttons and lights. Some had numbered stickers beside the buttons, but others had no stickers at all. It was clearly a work in progress.

My curiosity spurred me on to press a button to see if it made any of the lights across the top light up. The first button I pushed had a 1 beside it, and when I pressed it, a blue light at the top flashed. I pressed 4. Another light flashed. I pressed an unmarked button, and nothing happened. I pressed zero, and another light flashed. Then

I pressed another unmarked button.

To my surprise, lights on the floor that circled the podium and most of the small room lit up and began flashing.

"What on Earth is he making?" It made no sense to me. I hoped I didn't break it by pressing buttons. I looked for an off switch, but there was nothing on the podium except a small lever on the side. "Maybe this is the off switch," I mused aloud and pushed it down.

Instantly I was engulfed in a white light that shot up from the circle surrounding me and filled the room. I felt a weird electrical energy shoot through me and then everything went black.

Chapter 6

When I opened my eyes, I was outside. I slapped away the tall grass that tickled my cheek. My mind scrambled to remember who I was and where I was. It took a moment for it all to come back to me. *Uncle Charlie's house!*

"Oh my god!" I shrieked, crawling to my feet. The house was gone! The house, his car, his garage, everything! Gone! "What have I done?" And then a more disturbing thought filled my mind. "What was Uncle Charlie working on?" *Could he have really been building a nuclear bomb?* Had I just wiped out his entire property with a bomb?

But then I realized that a bomb would've likely killed me. Although it had thrown me far enough that the road was just a few feet from me. *Was I dead and now in some sort of Heaven with miles of tall grass?* I was more of a city girl, so miles of farmland would not be considered my idea of Heaven.

"My purse!" I saw the glint from the chain on the strap of my shoulder bag. I hurried to pick it up and rummaged through it for my phone. "I need to call Neil!" It was telling that the first person I thought to contact, in whatever disaster I might find myself in, was Neil. By all rights, I should've tried to call Uncle Charlie to tell him I'd just accidentally blown his house up.

No signal. *Rats!*

Then I realized that *my* car was also gone. I'd have to walk home, but I felt weak and doubted I would make it. I struggled just to walk a few feet, so two miles was out of the question. *Maybe I just need a rest,* I told myself and sat back down on the grass.

Uncle Charlie would have to come home eventually, and when he did, I'd tell him what happened and maybe he could call a taxi for me or something.

I rested my head on my knees and tried to figure out what had happened until I heard horse hooves that startled me. Horses in Weaverton? I had never seen anyone with a horse in Weaverton. *Had Uncle Charlie traded in his three-wheel bicycle for a horse?*

I stood, and my legs gave out, forcing me to sit back down. It was then that I noticed that I'd somehow wiped out *all* the houses across the road from Uncle Charlie as well.

I was surprised to see three men on horseback approaching, looking pretty much like cowboys from the wild west. *What is going on?* I wondered. Was there some sort of parade or something that I didn't know about?

They stopped and all three men stared at me. *They must've heard the blast,* I guessed.

"You okay?" The first guy asked. "What happened to you?"

"I, uh," I stammered, not wanting to admit to a total stranger what I'd just done. "I have no cell phone signal." He squinted at me making me feel even more uncomfortable. "Could you call a taxi for me?"

"A what, now?" he asked. He looked at his two friends behind him. They all shrugged their shoulders but remained silent. "Come again?"

"Um, my uncle's house is gone," I said, pointing at the field behind me. "I take it you're on your way to an event or something, but if you could just take a minute to call a taxi for me, I would appreciate it."

"Are you okay?" he asked again, dismounting and walking slowly towards me. His unshaven face and his dirty pants gave him an aura of authenticity that I'd never seen in any parade. "I don't understand what you're saying. Did you get hit on the head or something?"

My words sounded normal to me, I thought.

"Am I speaking gibberish?" I wondered aloud as he walked closer to me, eyeing me up and down.

"Kinda," he said, looking confused. "Look, ma'am, I don't know what you're asking for, or where you came from, but are you out here all by yourself?"

His friends looked dirty and grimy, possibly even dangerous. Admitting that I was out here all by myself might not be the wisest thing to do.

"My uncle will be here any second," I said. "Or a car will come by soon. You should probably just continue on your way so that you won't be late."

"Late for what?" he asked. Even in the shade of the brim of his dusty cowboy hat, I could see the confusion in his blue eyes.

"Well, you're obviously going somewhere," I said, pointing at the other two on horseback. "Don't let me stop you."

"Yeah, Carter, come on, we gotta go," one of his friends said and spit tobacco on the ground. *Gross!*

"We can't just leave her out here," Carter said to his friend.

"Well, we can't take her with us!" his friend argued.

"Did your horse get away?" Carter turned to me again.

"No, I didn't have a horse," I said, confused by his question.

"How did you get out here?" he asked, looking around. "Guys, this might be an ambush."

"I drove!" I said. "In my car!"

"In your cart? Without a horse?" Carter asked.

"No, *car*, not cart!" I explained. *What is wrong with him?*

"Okay, ma'am, you're talking gibberish again," Carter said, holding up a hand. "You must've been out in the sun too long or something. Can I help you get somewhere?"

"Carter!" his other friend yelled. "We have to go now!"

Carter pinched his lips together. "It's miles from nowhere, and there's clearly something wrong with her. We can't just *leave* her."

"Carter, you don't need *another* woman!" his friend yelled, clearly frustrated.

"Okay, listen, you guys go on," Carter told them. "I'll meet you at the falls tomorrow. I'm not just gonna leave this poor little woman here all by herself. I'll take her back to Weaver Settlement and catch up with you guys tomorrow!"

"No, I need to get into town," I insisted, standing and hoisting my purse on my shoulder. "Weaverton."

"Sorry, ma'am," Carter said as his friends shook their heads and rode off at full gallop down the road. "I don't know where that is. The nearest town is Weaver Settlement."

"Is it that way?" I pointed towards Weaverton.

"Yup," he said, mounting his horse and reaching down a hand. "Come on."

I rapidly debated my options. For all I knew, this could end up being the only opportunity I'd have to get back into town. I considered the possibility that the next group of guys heading to whatever event they were participating in wouldn't be as nice as this guy.

I grasped his waiting hand, and he pulled me up behind him and turned his horse around, facing town. Maybe he was trying to stick to character by calling Weaverton by an old name.

"So, what's your name?" he asked as we rode. "Mine's Carter. Carter Richards."

"I'm Taylor," I told him. "Taylor Cooper."

"Taylor? That's an odd name," Carter said. "For a girl."

"No, it isn't," I said. "Plenty of people are named Taylor."

"For a *first* name?" he asked. I could hear the skepticism in his voice.

"Yes, of course," I said. "Haven't you ever heard of a certain famous singer named Taylor?"

He let out a hearty laugh. "A famous singer? Why, do *you* sing?"

"No," I admitted.

He chuckled silently as we rode. I was surprised that he didn't even ask why all of the houses on the road had disappeared.

But then I noticed more anomalies. The road had

been paved this morning, and now it was just a gravel road that stretched out in both directions. I noticed another disturbing thing; there were no telephone poles. *There was no way I could've blown up a house, the neighbors, and the pavement off the roads and still left the trees standing!*

What had my uncle been inventing? Had he sent me into an alternate dimension?

When we approached town, which turned out to be a dusty town straight out of the pioneer books, complete with horses, wagons, and people in pioneer clothes, I had to ask the question. "Carter?"

"Mhm?" he mumbled as we rode into the dusty town.

"What year is it?" I asked softly, not sure I wanted to know the answer.

He gave another hearty laugh. "Did you get hit on the head?" he asked. "It's 1884!"

"1884?" I shrieked. "It can't be! I can't be in 1884! How did this happen?"

He swung his leg over the front of the horse and jumped to the ground. "Come here," he said, reaching up and grabbing me by the waist, helping me to the ground.

My legs trembled, and I wondered if I would faint. "It can't be 1884."

"Why, Miss Taylor?" Carter asked, looking into my eyes with a serious expression. "What year do *you* think it is?"

"It's 2024!" I said, but I was genuinely doubting myself now. "Is this some kind of joke? Please, if this is some kind of cosplay or something, don't mess with my head!"

"What the heck is cosplay?" Carter asked, slapping his hand against my forehead. "You don't have a fever. Come with me."

He grabbed me by the wrist and dragged me along behind him down the dusty street. I accidentally stepped in horse manure in my good sneakers! "Stop!" I yelled. "I just stepped in horse crap!"

He stopped and looked at me and then down at my shoes. His expression was even more confused. "What kinda boots are those?"

"They're sneakers," I said. "Look, I don't know how my uncle's machine zapped me to wherever this is, but I just need to get to a pay phone or something, or the next town."

He scowled at me. "You should be wearing boots," was all he said before continuing to drag me along behind him and into a shed-like building with a sign that read Doctor above the wooden door.

An older gentleman with barely any hair and small wire-rimmed glasses looked up from a desk. "Carter, you better get out of here. The sheriff's looking for you."

"I know, Doc," Carter said. "It's just a small misunderstanding that I'm gonna clear up."

The doctor turned his attention to me. "Who do we have here?"

"I found this woman out on the trail to the falls," Carter explained. "I couldn't just leave her."

"I'll take care of her, but seriously, Carter, you gotta go, now!" the doctor said.

"Take care, ma'am," Carter said to me, tipping his hat and running out.

"So, what seems to be the problem, ma'am?" the doctor asked.

"You can call me Taylor," I said.

"That's an unusual name," he said, eyeing me up and down the way the cowboys had. "Where are you from?"

"Weaverton," I said.

"Never heard of it," the doctor said. "I'm Ephraim Walker, you can call me Doc."

"Okay, Doc," I said. "I have no idea what's going on here. I somehow got zapped here, well, a few miles out of town, and my cell phone isn't working."

"Cell phone?" Doc asked. "I'm sorry, I don't understand."

"Are you for real?" I asked. "Is this some sort of cosplay? Or did my uncle actually build a time machine and send me back to 1884?"

"Cosplay?" he asked with the exact same expression that Carter had when I'd asked him.

"Yeah, you know, pretend it's 1884," I said. "Costumes, town, everything?"

"Did you hit your head?" he asked. "Cover your eyes."

I did as I was told, thinking how absurd this entire day was. He pulled one of my hands away from my eye and peered into it. Then he did the other.

"You don't seem to have a concussion," he said.

"There's nothing wrong with *me!*" I insisted. "Look, I'm sorry for ruining 1884 for you, but I really need to get home. I have three kids! If you have any kind of a phone I can use to at least call them, please let me use it."

"I've heard of them, but I've never seen one," Doc said. "Listen, there's a stagecoach that comes by in the morning. It'll take you to Harper Falls. It's a bigger town and maybe you can find your way home from there."

"So, that's how I get out of this, whatever this is?" I asked. "You get in and out of the cosplay by a stagecoach?"

"I'm sorry, I don't understand what you're trying to say, but the coach will get you to the next town in the morning," he said. "Meanwhile, I take it you don't have a place to stay for the night?"

"The night?" I shrieked. "I have to get home to my kids!"

"Is anyone with them?" he asked.

"My husband," I said.

"How did you get so far away from home?" he asked.

"I don't know!" I shrieked.

"Okay, how about you stay at my place tonight?" he offered. "My wife would love to have you."

"You guys stay here all night?" I asked in amazement, refusing to admit that somehow it was *really* 1884. "Can't you call the stagecoach now?"

He squinted at me. "Perhaps you better lie down for a while. Please, come with me."

Because he was old and seemed kind, I trusted him and followed him through the back of his office and into a narrow hallway with ancient but well-kept wallpaper. He led me up a narrow wooden staircase with a shiny mahogany banister.

"Mary! We have a guest for the night!" he announced when we reached the top of the stairs that opened into a wide living room.

A middle-aged woman, plump and smiling, emerged from the kitchen. "Oh, welcome! Welcome!" she said. "You're just in time! We're having wild turkey and potatoes!"

"Mary, show her to the guest room, I think she should lie down for a while," he said.

"I'm fine," I insisted.

"Well, I'll show you where the guest room is anyway," Mary insisted. "What's your name, dear?"

"Taylor," I said.

"Oh my, that's an unusual name for a girl," she said. "Do you have any clothes?"

"Just these," I said. "I only planned to be gone for the day."

"Okay, well, you can wear one of my nightgowns tonight," she said. She led me into a small but clean bedroom with white linen blankets. The same fleur-de-lis pattern in green and purple covered the walls with white wainscotting along the bottom. "This is where you'll sleep, dear. The lavatory is downstairs if you'd like to go get washed up for dinner. It's just at the bottom of the stairs."

The vision of a bathroom which I had in my head paled in comparison to the glorified indoor outhouse I discovered at the bottom of the stairs. I lifted the wooden toilet seat and peered in to see a can far below. *Someone must empty it from the back of the building,* I surmised.

The only source of water in the bathroom was a pitcher of cold water and a porcelain bowl on a small wooden table. I poured a little in the bowl and washed my face with my hands and then dried off with the thin linen towel that hung above the table. There was nothing to drain the water into, and I didn't know if I should dump it into the toilet or not, so I just left it. I cringed at being a bad houseguest, but *seriously*, they could at least have had a regular bathroom.

Dinner was delicious, and Ephraim and Mary proved to be great company. They told me stories of their lives and the town. I listened with interest, thinking that these people were very committed if this *was* just a cosplay. I could not bring myself to consider the alternative.

When dinner was over, I was full and tired. "Let me do the dishes," I offered, beginning to clear the table.

"You'll do no such thing, dear," Mary said, taking the dish from me. "You're our guest."

After an evening of tea and good conversation, I lay in bed, which for all its shabby chic beauty was uncomfortable, and thought about the day. *Was this real? Had I really time traveled? Or was this just some elaborate multi-day cosplay that I'd stumbled into? But what had happened to Uncle Charlie and his house? And his neighbors?*

I struggled to make sense of what was happening and sometime after roosters started crowing in the distance, I fell asleep.

Chapter 7

In the morning, after a hearty breakfast of bacon, eggs, rolls, and milk, Mary walked me down to the stagecoach station.

"If you ever come back this way again, don't forget to drop in," Mary said, giving me a hug. "Do you have the fare for the stagecoach?"

"I don't have much cash on me," I said. "I only have about $20."

"That's plenty!" Mary exclaimed. "It's only four to go to Harper Falls."

"Whew," I said. "I can manage that."

But I wasn't expecting the problem I encountered when I tried to buy my ticket. "That's fake," the guy behind the ticket counter said flatly and slid it back to me.

"No, it's not!" I insisted. "Are you serious? You are not going to take modern cash?"

"If modern is the new word for counterfeit, then yes, I'm serious," he said. "Dan, go get the sheriff!"

"I'll pay for her," Mary spoke up behind me and snatched my twenty from the counter, pushing it into my hand quickly. She rummaged in her tiny purse with a chain handle and pulled out the money.

"Thank you," I said, offering her the twenty in exchange. "I didn't know you guys take it so far."

She looked confused and pushed my hand away.

"No, I don't want that," she said. "I don't know what you and that Carter boy are up to, but it's best if you get yourself as far away from him as possible. He's nothing but trouble. He's gonna get himself hanged one of these days."

"Well, that's a bit extreme," I said. "But I only met him yesterday when he found me on the road and gave me a ride here. I don't really know him."

"Well, just watch out for him," she said. "Now, you take care, you hear?" She gave me another hug.

I climbed into the stagecoach, feeling a bit out of place in my jeans with everyone else in full 1884 costumes. A man with a black beard and handlebar mustache sat across from me with a younger man about my age, who was all dressed in black. Another man, with long black hair, who was also dressed in black, climbed in beside me. I wanted to pull out my phone and continue reading an eBook I'd started ages ago but hadn't found time to finish. An eight-hour carriage ride would be the perfect time to read, but somehow, it didn't seem appropriate to pull out a modern device. Besides, these guys looked like they took their cosplay a little too seriously.

Somewhere in the back of my mind was the disturbing notion that perhaps this *wasn't* some cosplay. Perhaps my uncle's invention had indeed been a time machine, and I was actually in the year 1884! I figured I'd wait and see what I could find out when I reached Harper Falls.

Chapter 8

Despite the appearance of cushioned seats, the ride was bumpy. Continuously! Even if I'd wanted to have some sort of conversation, it would've been difficult by the loud crunching of wheels on gravel and the harness and hooves of four horses.

After about fifteen minutes of regretting this journey because of the way all three men kept staring at me, the men began talking amongst themselves. If they'd been trying to have a private conversation, the need for speaking loudly to be heard made privacy impossible, so I pretended to sleep.

"Are you sure Jake's meeting us there?" the younger guy across from me asked.

"If he knows what's good for him, he will!" the older guy across from me with the handlebar mustache answered.

"I don't think we can trust him," the guy beside me said.

"Then trust me!" the older guy said. "I said he'd be there, and he'll be there! Son of a bi—" His words were cut off by loud gunshots on either side of the carriage.

I sat upright and peered out the window. Several masked men on either side of us rode along firing guns. I held my breath and willed the driver to outrun them. I became even more alarmed when all three men inside the carriage whipped out guns from their holsters. Staring at them closeup, I realized this was *not* cosplay. These guns were for real, and I could just feel the evil in the air.

My breath froze in my throat, and despite believing that my heart would stop, it pounded louder than ever in my ears. When I heard the driver shout at his horses, "Woah! Woah!" and the hooves slowed, I panicked. *So, this is how I die. In some western gunfight.*

"Get out!" A guy wearing a handkerchief over his face swung the door beside me open. "Hands up!"

The guy behind me shoved me out of the way and shot at the guy that had ordered us out. "Oh!" The guy outside yelled and fell back against the carriage. Just then the door on the other side of the carriage opened and the guy behind me with the gun was yanked out. In seconds, another masked man was on my side of the carriage. "Get out!" he yelled and grabbed my arm, pulling me down from the carriage.

"Drop your guns!" A third masked man yelled as he stepped out of the bushes with two more guys with their faces covered. "Now!" He shot into the air. The three men that had been inside the carriage with me threw their guns on the ground, and to my surprise, the three that had ordered us out of the carriage also threw *their* guns on the ground.

The new guy held the gun on us while his two friends came over and tied up the men, *all of them* except the coach driver, emptied their pockets, and then picked up the guns from the ground.

"Sorry, ma'am," one of the new guys said to me, looking me straight in the eyes. His voice sounded familiar, and I realized it was Carter.

"Car—" I started to say, but he put a finger to my lips and winked.

"Shh," he said. "Ma'am, I apologize for this interruption in your journey."

He offered his hand to help me back into the coach.

"On your way, driver!" Carter shouted, then he turned to the other guys that his friends had tied up. "You guys are comin' with me!"

I didn't realize I was trembling until the carriage started moving again. *Mary was right! Carter is bad news! But why had he not even tried to rob me?* As I thought about it, I realized he didn't even touch any of the luggage piled on the back and on top of the coach. He'd just wanted the men! Were they part of his gang or something? But then again, if they were his friends, there were easier ways to contact them!

After we'd traveled about ten minutes, the coach stopped again. I nervously peered out of the windows. *Are we being robbed again?* I'd been traumatized.

The driver jumped down and came around and opened the door. "Ma'am are you okay?" he asked.

I nodded. "I think so," I said. "Does this happen often?"

"Only when I'm carrying a trunk of cash for the bank," he said, nodding towards the back.

"But they didn't take it," I said.

"Thanks to Carter Richards," the driver said. "He knows that on the first Sunday of every month I transport the cash from the bank in Weaver Settlement to the bank in Harper Falls. He's saved a few of the deliveries."

"So, he's a *good* guy?" I asked.

"I suppose he's as good as can be after being framed for a bank robbery," the driver said. "That might be why he wanted those guys."

What he said made no sense to me, but I was still shaken up from the robbery, or robbery prevention.

"So, which guys were the robbers?" I asked. "The guys in the coach, or the guys that pulled us over?"

"All of them," he said. "But don't you worry none; Carter will be riding along the trails beside the road."

I nodded and briefly wondered if I'd somehow fallen in my uncle's basement and hit my head, and this was some kind of unconscious dream or something.

"If you're alright then, we'll carry on," the driver said.

As the driver had promised, there were no more incidents along the way, and we reached Harper Falls by suppertime.

My legs were stiff and achy when I crawled from the stagecoach. I surveyed my new environment. Harper Falls was considerably bigger than Weaver Settlement. There were horses and wagons everywhere tied to posts.

There was a post office and a bank beside the stagecoach station, and a hotel on the other side of that. Between the stagecoach station and the post office was a street that ran up to a schoolhouse with a little white cottage beside it. Across the street were a saloon, a restaurant with a wide wraparound verandah, and a long red mercantile store with a huge sign that read Bell's Mercantile. Beyond that, a railroad track ran across the top of the hill. I could see the top of the railroad station behind the mercantile.

At the bottom of the hill, on either side of the road were a couple tiny shops, and then a green covered bridge that spanned a river. I could see on the other side, the road inclined again with huge houses on either side. I couldn't see, from where I stood, what lay beyond the trees at the top of that hill.

I was now faced with a new problem. I had no 1884 money! I didn't even have any belongings that I could trade. The only things I had in my purse were my cell phone and a solar-charged power bank, a notebook and pen, some makeup, a grocery list, and a losing lottery ticket besides my wallet that contained useless credit and debit cards and cash from the future.

I bravely walked into The Falls Grand Hotel. The heavy wooden double-doors led me into a large room with hardwood floors, waxed and shiny, reminding me of a school gym, although more in the condition at the end of a school year than at the beginning. I walked up to the large wooden counter and rang the little bell.

"One moment!" A sweet female voice shouted from beyond a door behind the counter. Soon, a twenty-something girl with her hair up in a bun emerged with a wide smile. "Hello, and welcome to The Falls Grand Hotel, my name is Annie! Will you be staying with your husband?"

"My husband?" I asked in confusion.

She nodded at my wedding ring as she grabbed a pen and dipped it in a jar of ink.

"Oh, no, he couldn't make it," I said. "I've come alone. Could you please tell me what your rates are?"

"$2 a night," she said sweetly.

"$2?" I asked in surprise. I imagined such a large hotel would charge more.

"Well, yes, but there *is* a flushing bathroom on each floor," she said.

"Oh," I said in surprise. "$2 is a good price!" I assured her.

"How many nights will you be staying?" she asked, pen poised and ready to write.

"Well, I'm not exactly sure yet," I said. "I seem to be stranded. And I won't have any money until I can get to the bank tomorrow." *If I can manage to get a bank loan,* I thought. I assumed banks were more lenient about loans in 1884 because everything was so cheap.

"That will be no problem," she said. "I can give you a room for a week, and then we can book for another week if you decide to stay longer. Could I have your name please?"

"Taylor," I said. "Taylor Cooper."

"That's a nice name," Annie said, looking at me with a wide smile. "I've never heard that name as a first name before."

"Really?" I asked in surprise.

She nodded. "I think you'll like Harper Falls," she said. "Come, I'll show you to your room. I can have Lawrence carry your bags. Lawrence!"

"Oh, I don't have any," I said.

"You don't have any luggage at all?" she asked in surprise.

"As I said, I kinda got stranded here," I said. "I don't have anything with me."

"Well, I have some dresses that would probably fit you," she offered. "If you'd like to get out of those

56

men's clothes."

"Men's clothes?" I asked. She looked at my jeans with a grimace.

"Unless you'd like me to get some clothes from Lawrence?" she looked confused.

"No, no, dresses are fine," I said. "It's a long story, but I ended up here by accident. I'm stranded and, to be honest, I'm not even sure where *here* is."

"Harper Falls," she said, eyeing me like I somehow had forgotten the name of the town and sign.

"Yes, I know," I assured her. "I mean, I got lost, and . . . lost my way." It was a hopeless case, and after seeing real blood in a real gunfight, I was not going to divulge to anyone else that I was from the future.

"Well, the townsfolk here are very friendly," she said. "I'll put the word out and get some things for you."

"Oh, thank you so much!" I said. "You are so kind."

"It's my pleasure," she said, swinging open a white door. "Welcome to Harper Falls!"

I stepped into my room. It was quite large with a large, canopied bed. A table beside the bed held a kerosine lamp and a box of matches. A table near the door held a pink-flowered porcelain basin with a matching pitcher filled with water. A large square block of brown soap rested on a folded white linen towel. Other than a rocking chair by a window and a large oval braided rug, the room was pretty sparse.

"We have a library down the hall," Annie said, pointing to an archway at the end of the hall. "I'm sorry, but I'm expecting the new schoolteacher to arrive on the train, so I must go. But is there anything else I can get you?"

"I really need to eat," I said, hoping she would tell me that there was some sort of cafeteria or something in the hotel.

"There is a restaurant across the street," she said. "Oh, but you don't have any money until tomorrow. I can talk to Mabel and have her add your meals to our hotel bill, how about that?"

"Oh, *could* you?" I asked in amazement. "That is so incredibly kind of you! How can I thank you?"

"It's no problem," Annie said with a smile. "We often do it for our guests. Just tell Mabel that I said to put it on the hotel bill."

"Thank you," I said again.

Just then the train whistle blew in the distance.

"I'm sorry, I'm supposed to meet the teacher at the train station," she said. "Enjoy your dinner."

"Thank you," I repeated as she hurried off. I followed her down the stairs and across the street.

I had to wait for a passing horse and buggy before I could maneuver my way around the horse manure and across the street. Tiny bells on the door rang as soon as I stepped into the restaurant. Several couples and a couple of men dressed in black, like the guys on the stagecoach eyed me up and down. I realized how out of place my attire was. I tried not to let my self-consciousness turn me around.

In a few seconds, a middle-aged Chinese lady came out of the kitchen and stared at me.

"I'm looking for Mabel," I said.

"I'm Mabo," she insisted. Her accent was heavy.

"Mabel?" I repeated.

"Mabo," she said. "Mabo. Not Mabel."

"Oh, I'm sorry," I said. I felt my face grow hot in embarrassment. "I'm sorry, I misunderstood Annie. She sent me here and said—"

"Put it on her bill," Mabo said. "Put it on her bill! Sit! Sit!"

She waved her hand indicating I could sit wherever I wanted. At least that's what I hoped she meant. I pulled out a heavy wooden chair and sat, admiring the beige linen tablecloths. I was impressed with how everything was so *authentic,* 100% cotton.

"Menu," Mabo said as she returned and handed me a thick paper menu. "You eat alone?"

"Yes," I said. I fought the urge to explain myself. Why I was alone. Why I was dressed so oddly. I quickly glanced at the menu while she stood and waited. "I'll have the chicken dinner," I said.

In a surprising short time, Mabo delivered a plate with two boiled potatoes, a side of brown beans, and two slices of chicken with gravy on them. She brought a glass of clear water and put it beside my plate.

"You like tea?" she asked.

"Yes, please," I said. I hadn't really been a fan of tea back home, but I was willing to try it.

When I was finished eating, I returned to the hotel, pondering my options. *If I'm going to be stuck in 1884, I'm going to need to get a job or something,* I figured. I had no idea what kind of job I could get. I wasn't qualified to do anything except marketing, and I couldn't imagine there being a great need for that here.

With the sun setting, the inside of the hotel was dim, but lamps lit the lobby and the hallways. I could see the glimmer of the lamp in the library at the end of the hall when I reached my door. I had no idea how to light the lamp in my room, but it couldn't be that hard. To my surprise, it was already lit. Annie must've done it.

I pulled out my phone, thinking maybe I would read until I was tired enough to go to bed, but when I saw my screensaver of my kids, I felt my heart break. I missed them so much, and I was flooded with guilt because I hadn't even thought of them all during the day. Granted, I'd been robbed at gunpoint on a stagecoach, or observed a robbery, or a kidnapping, or something. Then I'd had to deal with immediate needs. But the old familiar guilt pangs hit me hard. *I'm a horrible mother!*

I wondered what Neil was thinking now. *He must be wondering why I'm not home.* I opened the messages. Our last texts were about him forgetting to pick up Emily. That seemed so long ago and far away.

"I have to stop this!" I told myself, turning off my phone and putting it back into my purse. I had too much to deal with at the moment to indulge in feelings of guilt and regret. I couldn't be with my kids; there was nothing I could do about that. I had to make the best of it until I could figure out a way to get back home, or until Uncle Charlie could figure out what had happened and come to rescue me. I clung to that possibility for the moment. It was all I had.

I decided that reading a contemporary book would be my best bet to understand the current customs and lifestyle. I'd never been interested in history before, only the future. Other than to dwell on my own past and poor judgment.

When I reached the library, I was startled to see a

bespectacled man about my age with brown hair reading in an armchair beside the lamp.

He looked up, pushed his long hair out of his eyes, and gave me a pleasant smile.

"Oh, I'm sorry," I said. "I didn't know anyone was in here."

"Hello, I'm Daniel," he said and stood up. "I'm the new schoolteacher here. There are plenty of chairs." He gestured towards a matching armchair on the other side of the table with the lamp.

"Hi," I said. "I'm Taylor."

"It's nice to meet you, Taylor," he said. "Are you a guest at the hotel, or a relative of Annie's?"

"A guest," I said. "I kind of got stranded. Hence, my clothing." I gestured towards my jeans. He just smiled.

"Are you moving here, or just visiting?" he asked. "And how did you get stranded?"

"Well, *that's* a long story," I said.

He closed his book and gave me a warm smile. "I like stories," he said. "But if you prefer to not share it, that's okay."

"Not yet," I said. "It was just a disaster, and I think everything will be fine from here on out. I'm just hoping my uncle can find out where I am and rescue me."

"Oh?" he said with a nod of interest. "Were you on the wagon train heading west?"

"Uh, no," I said. "I was just trying to visit my uncle, but he wasn't home, and I ended up here. By accident."

"Wrong train?" he asked.

"Something like that," I said dismally.

"Well, I like to think everything happens for a reason," he said with a smile. "If you hadn't gotten on the wrong train, we never would've met, and now I have another friend in Harper Falls. And you do too!"

I smiled for the first time in ages. "Well, thank you," I said. "I needed a friend."

"Me too," he whispered. "But don't tell anyone."

"So, how did you end up here?" I asked him. "You obviously came here on purpose."

"Yes," he said with a nod and a grin. "When I was small, my family used to live here. I was about five when we headed west. My father got gold fever and decided it would be best for us. I always knew that I wanted to come back here someday, so last summer, I came back for a visit. When I found out the teacher here had gotten married and moved away, I applied for the job and got it."

"Oh," I said. "What happened to the classes she was teaching?"

He squinted at me for a second before answering. "Well, the school stayed closed for most of September, and then the ladies from the church filled in, taking turns. Then school was out for the weeks of the harvest. During the winter, school became difficult to get to for the children that lived outside of town, so it was closed until just recently. Pastor Ryan has been teaching for the past few weeks, and I start tomorrow."

"Well, congratulations!" I said. "Is it just a one-room schoolhouse?" I didn't want to sound like an idiot, but without the internet to answer these kinds of questions, I had no choice but to actually ask a human being.

"Yes," he said, and I appreciated that he didn't

make me feel stupid for asking.

We spent the next hour or so talking about the town, and he filled me in on who was who that he knew of. "A lot of new people have moved here," he admitted. "And a lot of people that were here when I was a child have moved away. Even people that lived here when I was here last summer have moved on."

"I have a feeling I'll be staying a while," I said dismally.

"Me too," he said. "We can be new together."

Chapter 9

The following morning, after a gracious delivery of clothing from Annie, who'd taken up a collection from her relatives, I set off, in the most uncomfortable underwear on the planet, to the bank, hoping they would buy my wedding ring. It was a $250 ring, so with the gold rush going on, I imagined the value would be at least that in 1884 dollars. I was wrong.

"I'll give you $9.25," Mr. Wells, the bank manager said.

"$9.25?" I shrieked. "What are you talking about? That's fourteen-karat gold!"

"Fourteen?" he asked in shock.

"Yes!" I insisted, allowing him to roll it over in his greedy little fingers for a few more minutes. "Fourteen karat gold! How much will you give me for that?"

"Just a minute," he said, abruptly getting up and leaving the stuffy office with my ring. "Wait here."

In about five minutes, he came back. "Yes, indeed, it is fourteen karats!"

"So, how much will you give me now?" I asked.

"$3.25!" he said.

"What?" I shrieked. "I said it's fourteen karats!"

"I know," he said. "I thought it was twenty-four karats."

I sat back. "So, gold is only worth $3.25?" I was

completely disillusioned.

"Unless it's pure gold," he said. "This? $3.25. And I'm being generous!"

"Okay, I'll take it back," I said, taking it from his hand. "So, would you give me a bank loan?" I was already upset so my level of politeness had severely deteriorated.

"Excuse me?" he asked. "Now, what do you want a loan for?"

"To live," I said. "To pay for my hotel room and meals."

"You want a bank loan to pay for a hotel room?" Mr. Wells asked with an astonished look on his face. "Well, Miss Cooper, that is a first!"

Even to my own ears, my question sounded stupid.

"Fine," I said, throwing my ring in my purse and leaving.

"I need to get a job," I told Annie as soon as I reached the hotel. "Isn't there something I can do in the hotel?" I'd already asked Mabo, Mr. Wells, and the mercantile and they all had no ability to hire me.

"Sorry," Annie said. "But you know, I think Irene has been sick at the post office, maybe you could offer to fill in for a few days. It wouldn't be much, but it would be something."

So, I went to the post office. Behind a massive shiny wooden counter sat an old man with white hair.

"Hello there," he said in a hoarse voice. "You must be the new lady in town I've been hearing about."

"I am new," I admitted. "I'm in desperate need of a job. Probably temporary, but I'm stranded here, and I have no money."

"Well, Irene is out sick, and I don't have anyone to fill in for her," he said, looking grateful. "If you would like to fill in, it would be much appreciated. I'll pay you seventeen cents an hour. You only have to work from eight in the morning until noon, then you can go for lunch for an hour. You'll have to make sure the mail bags are ready for the train station by two. Clyde will come by and pick them up at two and bring in new mail from the afternoon train at four. You'll have to sort the incoming mail into those boxes up there. You can close at four, and make sure all mail heading west is left in the back porch before you leave. Clyde picks that up at seven in the morning."

"So, eight hours of work a day?" I asked.

"You don't get paid for lunch," he said. "You can take an hour from noon to one."

"Okay, thanks," I said.

"You can start right after lunch if you like. I'll show you the ropes. Come back here." He lifted up a leaf in the counter and ushered me into the inner workings of the post office.

"Now these boxes here are sorted in alphabetical order according to last name," he said, pointing to a row of square open boxes with letters in some of them. "So, all the As are in here, for example," he said, taking out several letters. "So, if Seth Anderson comes in for mail, you would go through this pile. Also, if Joseph Atkins comes in, his would be in here."

"I get it," I said. "Easy enough."

"Now, when someone mails a letter, when they pay you, you use this stamp right here to stamp the date on it. Then you put it in one of these bags here." He pointed to a row of brown woven sacks that had city names printed on them. "If you get letters that aren't addressed to any of these cities, you use this chart here, and it will tell you what bag it goes in. When it gets to the cities, it will be rerouted to the correct area near that city."

"Okay," I said. "No problem." My confidence surprised me, but after having worked in a hectic male dominated corporation, having my own little spot to do a clearly defined job was like a vacation.

"Okay, see you back here at one," he said. "Go have some lunch."

Chapter 10

I wanted to pull out my phone and calculate how much money I'd be earning for a week, and if my suspicions about 1884 medicine were correct, it could end up being a full-time job. *Didn't people die of a mere cold in the 19th century?* Not that I wished for anything bad on Irene!

Once I was seated in Mabo's, and after she'd taken my order for chicken soup and bread for lunch, I opened my purse on my lap and secretly used my phone to calculate my income. *At seventeen cents per hour for seven hours per day, times five days per week, that would add up to the grand total of $5.95. That wouldn't even pay for my hotel room!*

"Howdy, stranger!" A familiar voice caught me off guard, and I dropped my phone into my purse. It was Carter. "Mind if I sit?"

"Hi," I said, nodding at the chair. Despite the various opinions of others about him, it was a relief to see a familiar face. "What are you doing here?"

"Oh, now that I got that little misunderstanding with the law settled by turning in the guys that *actually* robbed the bank, I decided to settle down, buy me a nice little piece of land, find me a wife," he said with a slow drawl, leaning back in his chair, tipping his cowboy hat, and smiling so wide his dimples delved deep into his cheeks. "What are you up to? I see you found your clothes."

"Oh, Annie borrowed these for me," I explained. "I've been trying to find a job so I can pay my hotel bill."

"Ask Annie," he suggested. "She'll hire ya!"

"I did," I said. "And she can't. But I do have a temporary job at the post office. Although, that's not even going to pay me enough to pay my hotel bill. Especially with my meals."

"You could find yourself a fella and get married," he suggested with a coy smile and held up his hand as Mabo brought out my dinner. "Mabo! Could I get the usual?"

"Yes, Mr. Carter!" Mabo said with a broad smile, and she patted Carter on the shoulder affectionately. "Coming right up!"

"The usual?" I asked in surprise. "You come here often?"

"When I'm in town," he said. "Which is often because I live here now."

"Oh, the land, the wife," I said, nodding.

"Well, the land, so far," Carter said with a wide grin. "Still workin' on the wife part." He winked. "Unless *you're* interested."

"Well, besides the fact that your proposal lacks a little something in terms of what a woman wants," I said with a grin. "I'm afraid that's impossible. I won't be staying here that long. As soon as my uncle finds me and rescues me, I'll be going home."

"*Rescue* you?" he asked with a look of shock. "From *what?* From me? From this beautiful town?"

I shook my head. "No," I said. "From 1884!"

"I hear ya," Carter said, shaking his head slowly. "Whew, this year has already been tough, and it's only March!"

Mabo showed up with a gigantic plate of dark brown beans and bacon, with what looked like sausages. "Here you go, Mr. Carter!" Mabo said proudly as she set it in front of him.

"Now, that's what I'm talking about!" Carter said, flashing her his charming smile and hoisting his fork and knife over the sausages. *Charming? Did I just think he was charming?*

Okay, I've already been in 1884 too long! How am I thinking this rough-around-the-edges cowboy could be charming? Besides, I'm married! At least for a while.

I was interrupted from my inner mental scolding by Carter. "You're soup's getting cold."

I focused on my lunch.

When Carter stopped eating to take a breath, he asked, "So, that's a firm no on my proposal then?"

I nodded and ate my soup. He shrugged and went back to his food. "You're missing out," he said. "You'll change your mind when you see the house I'm building."

Was he serious? Was he really asking me to marry him? I'm married already! Then it hit me that while I'd been missing my kids so much, I hadn't thought of Neil at all. In fact, it was a relief to not have to deal with him. I didn't care where he was or who he was with. I only hoped he was taking good care of the kids.

"Well, thank you for having lunch with me," Carter said as soon as he'd finished. "But I got me a house to build!" He stood, tipped his hat, and left.

My soup was cold, but I finished it anyway. I was

going into debt for this meal, and I was going to enjoy it! As soon as I was finished, I went back to the post office.

"Oh, good, you're back!" The elderly gentleman was sitting on the steps waiting for me. "Here is the key. Remember, open at eight in the morning, and lock it when you leave for lunch. And remember to put the morning mail in the back porch. Clyde has a key for that."

I took the key and wondered if mail theft was a big thing in the 1800s. I hadn't considered that idea ever before in my life.

The afternoon was boring with only two people coming in to mail letters. I snuck my phone out of my purse and read an eBook for a while. Thankfully, I'd been more of a book buyer than a book reader because of my hectic future life, so I had enough unread books on my phone to get me to my *actual* future probably. While I'd always been prepared enough to keep a solar-powered charger in my purse, I didn't dare to actually set it out anywhere that would require me to explain the gadget. I knew the power bank was full, so I plugged my phone into it inside my purse. I'd find a way to recharge it later.

When Clyde brought back the mail, I sorted it into the boxes. The only name I recognized on an incoming letter was for Daniel. If it was indeed the same Daniel, his last name was Jones.

When the mail was sorted, I went back to secretly reading my book, holding it inside my purse. Reading helped the time pass and kept my mind off my kids. Ironically, appreciation of that fact took my mind straight back to the kids. I wondered if Neil had remembered to pick Emily up from daycare. I wondered how August and Amber had made out at school. *Was August doing his homework?*

"Hey there!" A cheerful voice shook me out of my worry, and I dropped my phone in my purse and put the bag on the floor. It was Daniel.

"Hi, Daniel! How was your first day of school?" I asked.

"It was great! The kids are amazing," he said. "There's one boy that's a handful, but I'm sure he'll come around."

I almost said *boys will be boys* but remembered how obnoxious I'd found it every time Neil had used it to dismiss August's bad behavior. "I'm sure you'll get through to him," I said, hoping it didn't sound dismissive.

"Did anything come in for me, by any chance?" he asked.

"That depends," I said. "I need to know your last name."

"Oh, I'm sorry," he said, blushing. "I thought I'd said when I met you. My last name is Jones. Daniel Jones."

"Then, yes, Daniel Jones," I said with a smile as I turned to retrieve the letter. "A letter did come in for you today."

"Thank you!" he said, staring at the envelope as soon as I handed it to him. "Thanks!"

"No problem," I said. "It's my job." I gave a little laugh. It felt weird to have such a mundane job. It was an important job, yet it was peaceful. If I ever got back to the future, I would consider the idea of quitting my hectic corporate job and just getting a job at a post office or something. At least I'd have experience, although no references a future boss could call.

Daniel turned to leave and then turned back, scrunching up his face as if what he was about to say was going to physically hurt to get out. "I was thinking," he pointed the envelope at me. "If you're going to be eating at Mabo's, and I'm going to be eating at Mabo's, why don't we just eat together?"

"Sure," I said. "I kind of hate eating alone."

"Me too!" he said, sounding amazed that we had something in common. "I'll see you there, then!" he said.

When he reached the door, he turned again. "What time?"

"When I'm done here at four," I said. I glanced at the pocket watch that swung from a chain on a hook by the counter. "Which is actually right now!" I laughed. "I guess I lost track of time."

"Okay, then!" Daniel said and waited at the door for me. I grabbed my bag and took the mail key from the hook beside the pocket watch.

After I locked the door, Daniel and I walked together down the street to the hotel. "I just have to drop off my books," he said. "I'll just be a minute."

I went inside and said hi to Annie. "You're sure you can't hire me?" I asked her.

"No, I'm sorry," she said. "But you know, it would be cheaper if you rented that house from Isaac Carpenter. He's taking his family and heading west. It's got 5 acres of land and ever since he got sick last year, he's been talking about how much better off he'd be in the gold in California. I hear he wants $10 a month for rent and you'll be able to pay it through the bank."

"Yes!" I said instantly.

"He's going to be passing through town in the morning," she said. "I'll bring him by the post office."

"Well, howdy!" Carter said cheerfully as he stepped into the hotel. I hated the way he set butterflies in motion in my stomach. "Fancy seeing you here!" His smile was disarming, and without choosing to, I felt my face break into a warm smile.

"Why, Mr. Carter, I do believe you're stalking me," I said in my best fake southern drawl.

"Or the other way around," he said back, eyeing me up and down in a way that made the hair stand up on my arms.

Just then Daniel came down the steps. "All ready!" he announced. "Shall we go?" He held out an elbow for me to put my hand through. I did and slightly enjoyed the look of shock on Carter's face.

"Well, now I know why you turned down my proposal!" Carter said.

Daniel froze and his face turned beet red. He looked at me, and all I could see on his face was fear. I wondered if he'd also been warned that Carter was dangerous.

"He's joking!" I told Daniel and shot Carter a look of exasperation that I hoped he couldn't tell wasn't legitimate.

By the time we crossed the street, Daniel's face had almost resumed its normal color.

"Carter has a weird sense of humor," I said, trying to put Daniel at ease.

"It's fine," Daniel said, shrugging like it didn't matter.

"So, I might be renting a house!" I told him as soon as we sat down. I figured changing the subject might put him more at ease.

"Wow, that's great!" he said. "I'll miss you at the hotel."

"I'll see you when you pick up your mail," I said. "Plus, I'll still have to come into town to buy groceries!"

"Oh," he said, looking surprised. "You're moving out of town?"

"Just outside of town," I said. "I have no idea exactly where, but I'll find out tomorrow."

"That's great," he said. "I'm happy for you, Taylor."

He sounded a little disappointed though.

In the morning, Annie brought Isaac Carpenter into the post office. Isaac looked tired, and his face was weathered.

"I'll tell you what," Isaac said in a deep growly voice. "You send me $10 a month and when you've paid me $300, the place is yours, free and clear!"

"What? Wow!" I was shocked. *$300?* "Thank you so much!"

"Just take it to the bank and they'll wire it to me," he said.

"Do we need to sign a contract?" I asked when he reached out to shake my hand.

Isaac shrugged. "My brother works at the bank, when it's all paid, he'll sign the deed over to you."

"I've known Isaac all my life," Annie vouched for him. "His word is better than gold!"

"Okay then," I said, shaking his hand vigorously.

"We have a deal?" he asked gruffly.

"We have a deal!" I said.

"You don't happen to want a cow, do you?" Isaac grumbled.

"How much?" I asked.

"$20," he said. "She won't make it out west."

"I don't have that much right now," I confessed.

"I'll add it onto the cost of the house," he said. "So, $320 and it's all yours, okay?"

"Thank you!" I said, realizing I was still shaking his hand. "Thank you so much, Mr. Carpenter!"

I wished him well on his journey and he left, giving Annie a hug before walking out the door and leaving us alone.

"Oh, this is so exciting!" Annie gushed, clasping her hands together. "I'm so happy you're staying!"

"Me too," I admitted. Somehow, despite missing my kids dreadfully, there was a peace in my heart that I hadn't felt in a long, long time.

Chapter 11

"So did you get your house?" Daniel asked me after school.

"Yes, I did!" I enthused. "And a cow!"

"Wow, lucky you!" Daniel said with a proud smile.

"Well, I haven't seen it yet," I admitted. "But Annie said she'd drive me out there after work."

"Congratulations," he said with a smile and shoved his round wire-rimmed glasses up on his nose.

"You're welcome to come see it with me," I said. "I'm sure Annie won't mind."

"Sure," he said with a grin. "I'd love to."

I was surprised to see that Isaac had left my cow tied up behind the hotel, where she'd been all day. Thankfully, she'd had grass to munch on. It was then that I realized I hadn't a clue how to look after a cow, much less milk her! And it wasn't like I could do an internet search for a video on how to do it. I didn't want to admit my lack of knowledge in front of Daniel and Annie, so I decided I'd probably figure it out. There must be books on the topic, I thought. Maybe I could admit my lack of skills to either Daniel *or* Annie, but not both. The cow walked beside the wagon and seemed to know her way home.

Much to my dismay, the little homestead was further outside of town than I'd imagined. "How will I get to work?" I asked Annie. "It will take at least an hour to walk into town."

"We don't really need to rent out your room yet," Annie said. "So, you could stay at the hotel for tonight. I won't charge you."

"Thank you," I said.

"And you only have one more day at the post office," she pointed out. "So, after that, it won't be a problem."

I was only hired for a week! I had allowed myself the delusional indulgence of fantasizing about the post office being a permanent job. Now I'd roped myself into some sort of mortgage and all I knew for sure I would be earning was $5.95!

"Have you heard how the regular post office lady is doing?" I asked.

"I haven't checked on her," Annie said. "But Irene's a tough old lady, and I'm sure she'll be back on her feet in no time. I'll ask around and let you know what I find out."

"Thanks," I said. "If I could keep this job for at least another week, at least that would pay for this house for a month." Which, ironically, I wouldn't be able to live in unless I bought a horse, and I had no idea what those would cost. "How much does a horse cost?" I asked.

"A good one is about $200 or $250," Daniel said.

I let out an exasperated sigh.

"Are there any other ways I could make money without having to go into town?" I asked.

"You could sell farm goods," Annie suggested.

"I'll think of something," I said, feeling the old

familiar stress and problem-solving gears kicking into high. *I've solved far more complicated problems at my future job!*

When we finally reached the little house, I was disappointed to see that it looked more like a shed. The exterior was made of dull gray boards with a tiny window on either side of the wooden slatted door.

"Oh, I forgot to get the key!" I exclaimed. "Oh, I'm so sorry for dragging you guys out here for nothing."

"There's no lock," Annie said with a little laugh and pushed the door open.

I followed her inside, thankful that the dimness of the ending day prevented her from seeing my red face. *How was I to know people didn't lock their doors in 1884?* I looked around and realized there was nothing anyone would steal.

A massive stone fireplace was in the very center of the small house, dividing it into two rooms. In the front room was a wooden table with a bench on either side and a wooden stool at either end. Over on the far wall was another small window. Beneath the bare window was another long wooden table with a porcelain basin and a red steel hand pump, leaving a bit of a sideboard on either end of the pump and basin. Beside that was a woodstove for cooking.

Beside the fireplace was a wooden ladder leading up to a loft, and behind the fireplace was a wooden bed with a grid of ropes strung across the frame but no mattress. The Carpenters must've taken it on their journey. They took *everything!*

I would have to make a note of everything I needed and then figure out a way to raise the money for it. I had no idea *how*, but I knew I *would,* because the only thing I did know with absolute certainty was that I had no choice!

Chapter 12

Late into the evening, I browsed every single bookshelf in the hotel library looking for information on how to raise cows and earn money. I wished I'd had the forethought to learn about this stuff when I'd had easy access to information.

"Finally!" I exclaimed much too loudly for the quietness of the evening. I pulled down a book that promised to instruct the American woman in everything from raising children to decorating a house and raising domestic animals!

"Ah," Carter said, stepping into the room out of nowhere. "We meet again!" He took long strides across the room and turned the cover of the book so he could see it. "I see you're preparing for marriage! Should I be happy?"

I rolled my eyes. "I have a cow," I said blankly and carried the book to the armchair.

"You do?" he asked, looking around.

"A cow and a house," I said. "I got it today from Isaac Carpenter."

"Ah, yeah, he said he was looking for someone to buy it," Carter said. "He offered it to me, but I already bought my own land."

"Lucky me," I said, and I meant it.

"So, why do you look so sad?" he asked. "Why,

it sounds like you have it all. A house, a cow, what more could you want?" His playful grin was enticing, but in the back of my mind, I knew I couldn't get attached. I would be going home eventually. And I was *married*, soon to be divorced, and had no intentions of making the same mistakes again!

"Well, the problem is, I have no idea how to raise a cow," I said. "Or for that matter how to even light a kerosine lamp."

His head whipped back, and his eyes widened. "Where on earth are you from, little lady?"

I sighed. "You wouldn't believe me if I told you," I said.

"Try me," he said. "Why, I know it ain't polite to ask a lady her age, but you look like you're almost my age. How is it you never learned how to light a lamp?"

In that moment, I was so tempted to tell him my secret. But, for all his charm and charisma, he didn't strike me as the kind of person that could be trusted with a secret.

"Never mind," I said. "I have some reading to do."

"Let me guess," he said. "You're a spoiled rich girl. The daughter of some tycoon. Maybe your daddy owns a gold mine, and you never had to work a day in your life."

"Far from it," I said.

"Hmm, okay, let's see," he followed me out of the library as I headed to my room. "You're a princess and on a royal tour of North America, you somehow got kidnapped and held for ransom. You ran away and got lost and that's when I found you." He grinned, obviously pleased with his theory.

"Wrong," I said. "*Very* wrong."

"Then why don't you tell me?" he asked. "It can't be that bad!"

"It's not bad," I said. "I just got separated from my uncle, and I have to wait until he finds me. Good night, Carter."

"Good night, princess," he said with a smile and a nod of his head. "In case you change your mind and want to share your mysterious past with me, I'll be right next door."

"Okay, I'll keep that in mind," I said. "Good night."

I closed the door and focused on my list of things I somehow had to figure out how to buy. I would need a kerosine lamp for the house, whether or not I knew how to light it. I would figure it out. It wasn't rocket science. I needed a mattress. Some food. I also needed more clothes. And a tub big enough to wash clothes in. And rope to put up a clothesline. The Carpenters had even taken their clothesline with them. The list didn't prove to be the distraction I'd hoped for, and I found myself thinking of Carter well into the wee hours of the morning.

In the morning, I went to work, and when Mr. Wells came in to check his mail just before lunch, I made a decision. "Here's your mail, Mr. Wells," I said, handing him a pile of envelopes. "I've reconsidered your offer, and I'm willing to take your offer on my gold ring."

He shrugged. "Bring it by my office," he said.

"I get off for lunch in a few minutes," I told him. "I don't suppose you're going back to the bank right now."

He twisted his jaw from one side to the other before answering. "No, I've got other matters to attend to," he said. "Let me see it."

I dug it out of my purse and handed it to him. He twisted his jaw again and scratched it, turning the ring over in his other hand. "I'll give you $3 for it." He finally said.

"Three?" I asked. "A few days ago, you said you'd give me $3.25!"

He rolled his eyes, sighed, and then counted out $3.25 from his pocket and put it on the counter. "Pleasure doing business with you."

Then I had an idea. It wasn't a good idea, and I knew I wouldn't follow through on it, but just for a moment, I indulged in the thought of *what if? What if I were to go to California, dig up some gold and take it back to the future with me?* This was instantly followed by the realization that I knew as much about gold digging as I did about cows.

Then there was the thought of a long journey without the use of airplanes. That didn't appeal to me, so I figured the next best thing I could do was find a way to earn money, buy as much gold as I could at the current price and take that back to the future with me! I'd be able to support my kids and not have to work at a job that was stressful, and I wouldn't need to stay with a cheating, unloving husband who I'd nearly already forgotten about!

By Friday, I had $9.20 to work with. It wasn't even enough to pay my rent. But I just knew if I could get at least one more week of work at the post office, it would buy me groceries and enough time to figure out what to do next! I wasn't sure when I would have to wire the rent to Isaac, but since he was going to California by wagon, it wasn't like he was going to arrive anytime soon.

I ate only a sandwich for lunch and just a bowl of soup for supper at the restaurant. I didn't want to rack up even more debt that I couldn't pay for a while. Annie was good about it and said I could pay her back whenever I could, but I knew I had to get into my own house as soon as possible. She hadn't been charging me for the room for the past few days, but I still had the bill coming from the restaurant of $3 a day. By Friday, I owed more than I had. I owed Annie $19.

When I left work on Friday, the old man came in and told me Irene would be out sick for one more week, and he would appreciate it if I could continue to fill in. I gladly accepted.

I headed straight for Bell's General Mercantile to get some food after a quick dinner with Daniel.

"I'm going to be moving out of the hotel soon," Daniel said.

"That's great!" I said. "I take it you have a house."

"Yes," he said, browsing the store while I shopped.

I was shocked that my entire basket of groceries came to 71 cents! For 71 cents, I got a pound of flour, a pound of sugar, a pound of coffee, a pound of rice, a pound of cheese, a pound of butter, and 20 apples.

Since I had a whopping $8.49 left, I spent $1 on a lantern and $6 on two blankets. For 10 cents, I bought a pound of tallow candles and a box of matches.

Annie drove me and my cow home, and Daniel

tagged along to help me carry all the stuff inside. Annie had loaned me a trunk to carry all the clothing she'd given me, as well as a cast-iron frying pan she said she could spare until I could get one. She also loaned me a mattress from one of the beds in the hotel. That would be the first thing I would buy with my next paycheck, I promised myself, because she looked a little worried as she loaned it to me.

"By the way, where can I buy a mattress?" I asked her. "I didn't see any at Mr. Bell's."

"You have to *make* them," she said, looking at me oddly.

"Right," I said, remembering she had no idea I was from the future. *I have to make a mattress.* I didn't want to ask how, but I hoped the book she'd let me bring home from her library would provide instructions.

"Remember, if you need anything at all, you let me know," Annie reminded me, while Daniel carried in wood and lit the fireplace for me. Then he lit the lamp for me and placed it on the table.

"Thank you for everything you've done for me," I said. "I don't know what I'd do without you."

"Well, you're like the sister I never had," she said and flung her arms around me in a hug.

I hugged her back. "You're like the sister I never had, too!" I said.

"Aw," Daniel said with a smile, wrapping his arms around the both of us. "And you're both like the sisters I already have, but miss," he said in a high-pitched voice. We all laughed and for the first time in years, I felt like I really had actual *friends!*

Chapter 13

I was glad it was Saturday the next day, and I could sleep in, but the roosters from some property beyond the hills apparently didn't care what day of the week it was because they began crowing somewhere around four in the morning.

I finally crawled out of bed because making an early cup of coffee was less annoying than trying to sleep with the constant raucous within hearing distance. Daniel had brought in wood for me the night before, so I put some in the cook stove, and tried to copy what Daniel had done when he'd lit a fire in the fireplace. I took some of the splinters off the edges of the wood and lit them first and then threw them into the wood section of the stove, throwing the match in behind it.

I got down the bags of sugar and the sealed box of Arbuckle's Ground Coffee, and the one tin cup and spoon that Annie had given me as a housewarming gift, and promptly realized that I had nothing to filter the coffee with. Then I realized that the stove fire had gone out. I restarted the fire and watched it until I was sure it was going to take this time, and then went back to my dilemma of the coffee filter. There was no way I was going to start this day this early without coffee!

I went and grabbed my phone off the roughly made wooden nightstand and checked the time. *How was it already 5:30?* Had it really just taken me an hour to get a fire going in the stove? How on earth was I to survive here?

"Okay," I said to myself. "I'm a problem-solver. How can I filter the coffee?"

I glanced around my bare kitchen, if I could indeed refer to it as a *kitchen*, and realized there was nothing to work with at all. I needed some kind of coffee filter. Not to mention a kettle. All I had to cook in was a cast-iron frying pan. I wondered how much water it could hold. It was pretty deep, so at least it should hold enough for one cup of coffee.

I decided that perhaps I could use the hotel towel that Annie had given me, but since it was the only one I had, I didn't want to ruin it. So, I slipped my bare feet into my sneakers and decided I would see if there had been any boxes of stuff left in the barn that might be of use to me. I hadn't even looked in the barn when I'd first visited the place. I hiked up my too-long nightgown and opened the door.

I was instantly met with a loud moo that scared the living daylights out of me. My cow filled my front door! I stumbled backwards and somehow prevented myself from falling. The cow walked right inside the house!

"No! No!" I shrieked. "Out, girl! Out!" I pointed to the door, but just like Stanley, the stray cat back home, she ignored me. Instead, she let out another series of moos that sounded so much louder in the house. I grabbed her by the rope around her neck and carefully turned her around, watching so she didn't touch the hot stove, and led her back outside in the dimly lit morning.

Her mooing continued as I led her around the back of the house.

She continued to moo at me while I led her back towards the field with the tall grass.

"Mornin', neighbor!" I jumped and turned around. There was Carter walking towards me with an amused grin. "Missing something? You're gonna need a bucket for that!"

"A bucket for what?" I asked.

He shook his head. "To milk the cow!" he said. "I could hear her mooing for the last five miles!"

"It wasn't her," I said.

He cocked his head sideways and pursed his lips as if he were dealing with a small child that had just been caught trying to do something ridiculous.

"Well, the last few were her," I admitted.

He walked closer and reached out his hand to the cow. "Easy, girl," he said. "What's her name?"

"I don't know," I said. "Isaac didn't tell me, and I was so excited about getting the house, I didn't really think to ask."

"Okay, well, I know you said you didn't know anything about cows, but I'll give you a hint," he said, rubbing his hand gently along her forehead. "If you milk her, she'll stop crying."

"Oh no!" I said. "With coming out here last night, I totally forgot to milk her in the evening!"

"I'll show you how to do it," he said. "I know cows."

"I *know* how to do it," I said. "Annie showed me. My cow has been staying behind the hotel for the last few days, and Annie showed me how to milk her."

He followed me into the house to get the bucket. "And do you always run around the yard with your cow in your nightgown?" he asked, chuckling under his breath.

"First time," I said. "I probably won't make a habit out of it."

"Do you need me to show you how to light your stove?" he asked with a wild grin.

"No thank you," I said pointedly. "I've already done that."

"I don't think so," he said. "There was no smoke coming out of your chimney!"

I walked to the stove and checked. Sure enough, it had gone out. "Crap!" I exclaimed. "I'll never figure this out! I don't belong here! I shouldn't have gone to my uncle's!"

"Now, now," Carter said, holding up his hands. "Calm down. I'm here to help."

"You came all the way out here to help me?" I asked in surprise. Carter was turning out to be a nice guy. It was true what the stagecoach driver had said about him. He was a good man.

"No," Carter said slowly. "I came all the way out here to go work on my house. I happened to hear your cow moaning from miles away and then saw you out running around in the mud in your nightgown. You obviously required my help, and being the knight in shining armor that I'm known for being, I graciously stopped to help you. Now, where's your bucket, and I'll milk the cow for you?"

"Thank you," I said, handing him the bucket off the bench by the table. "Here."

He nodded and took the bucket. And then both of us noticed my phone sitting on my kitchen table. I froze.

"What the heck is that thing?" he asked curiously, picking it up and turning it over and over in his hands.

"Okay, listen, I will explain everything," I said, snatching the phone from his hands. "But first, please just milk my cow for me. Then I will explain everything over a nice cup of coffee."

As soon as he went outside, I hurried into the back room and changed into my jeans and T-shirt. It was *my* home, and I could wear what I wanted. Especially if I had to come clean about being from the future. I knew he would think I was insane, but hopefully my futuristic clothing and gadgets would convince him. Heck, maybe he could even be instrumental in finding a way to get me back home again.

I tried to get the fire going, but still hadn't succeeded by the time Carter returned with the bucket of milk. It was only half-full. "I thought there'd be more," I said in surprise.

"Here, let me, ma'am," Carter said, giving me a gentle nudge aside as he approached the stove. "See this here thing up here on the pipe?" he pointed to a little iron handle thing. I nodded. "This here is the draught," he said. "Watch."

I watched as he lit a small bit of shaved bark and placed it gently in with the wood, then he slowly turned the little knob on the stovepipe. "It allows the air in."

I watched as the fire took off. "When you're done being amazed, would you like me to help you make coffee?"

"Oh, please do," I said. "I honestly don't know

what I'm doing." I tried not to show how close I was to the verge of tears.

He shook his head. "I see you haven't been reading that book on how to be a woman," he said. "I bet at home in your royal palace, you have hundreds of servants lighting fires and making coffee for you."

"Trust me," I said. "I did not come from a palace! And I certainly had no servants!"

"Well, if you read that book you had in the library, you'll learn," he said with a chuckle.

"I've been a little busy," I said.

"Running around with your cow in your nightgown," he said, still chuckling. "I know."

"I have an idea for a filter," I said.

"For what?" he asked.

"Coffee," I said.

He squinted and stared at me for a second and just shook his head.

"Do you have a kettle?" he asked.

"No," I said. "And I only have one cup, unfortunately."

"Who needs more than one?" he asked with a grin. "I came prepared, my lady!"

He rushed out the door and returned a few minutes later with a kettle and a cup.

"I guess you do come prepared," I said. "You carry a kettle and cup around with you all the time?"

"Every day when I go out to my property to work on my house," he said. "I start a little campfire, cook breakfast and everything."

"Resourceful," I said. I tried not to allow his tough-and-ruggedness to attract me. *I'm not staying in*

1884, I kept telling myself.

I pumped cold water into the kettle and set it on the stove. He went to shovel in some coffee. "What are you doing?" I shrieked, pulling his hand back. "We'll use filters!"

He carefully drew the little scoop back and dumped the coffee back into the tin. "Okay," he said slowly. "You can show me how they make coffee in the palace."

I took the coffee tin and put it on my side of the table and sat down to guard it.

"Okay, now, about that thing I saw on your table," he said. "Why don't you tell me what it is?" He sat down on the bench against the wall and leaned his elbows on the table across from me.

"Okay," I said slowly. "Are you sure you want to know? Once I tell you, I can't *untell* you. You might think differently about me."

"How do I think about you now?" he asked with a coy smile.

"All I'm saying," I said. "Is that our friendship might change."

"And you're saying you don't want it to?" he asked, folding his hands in front of him. "What is the big secret? What is it?"

"I have to make a filter!" I said, jumping up and running into the back room. My nightgown was too long for me anyhow, so I figured if I could take a few inches off the bottom of it, the linen would make a nice coffee filter. I'd have to use a hairband to secure it around the top of the cup, though. Since I would have to explain that, I knew that the time had come to let someone in on my secret.

"Okay," I said, emerging from the back room with the nightdress. I struggled to tear the bottom of the gown, but once I managed to tear the seam a few inches in, it was easy to tear several inches off the bottom in one long, even strip. I went back in the bedroom, threw what was left of my nightgown onto my bed and grabbed my bag.

"I'm pretty sure the kettle is boiling," he said, pointing to the stove.

"Okay," I said. I quickly secured a section of linen over the top of each cup with two hairbands, making extra sure they were completely clean with no hair or anything in them. I scooped some coffee into each makeshift filter and then poured the boiling water over them while he watched me carefully. I put the kettle back on the end of the stove.

"Quit stalling," he said slowly. He was more serious now.

I removed the filters.

"Sugar?" I asked. He shook his head, growing more serious by the second.

"Milk?" I asked.

He shook his head and silently watched me while I added a spoon full of sugar and scooped out a bit of cream off the top of the milk with a ladle and poured it into my coffee.

"Taylor!" he said. "Look, I've got a house to build. I don't know why you dress all funny, or what that weird square thing is that you wanted to hide so fast, but one thing I want you to know about me is I don't like games. If there is some huge secret you don't want to tell me, fine. I get it. You don't *have* to tell me anything. All I asked was what that weird thing was. You are free to tell me it's none of my business, and we can sit here and talk about cows, housebuilding, and post office work. Whatever you want. Just don't pretend to be so mysterious."

"I'm sorry, I'm not trying to be, honestly," I said. "What I'm about to say will surprise you, and you may not believe me, but here goes."

He took a sip of his coffee, sloshed it around in his mouth and waited.

"I'm from the future," I said.

He smiled and swallowed his coffee. He just stared at me, and I could tell he didn't believe me.

"Look, I know it's hard to believe," I said. "That's why I didn't want to tell anyone. But this," I said, pulling my phone out of my purse, "is a phone."

"A phone?" he asked, raising one eyebrow.

"Yes, look," I turned it on and watched his skepticism turn into curiosity. I flipped to the gallery and showed him pictures of my kids. "These are pictures of my kids."

"Holy crap!" he said, reaching for the phone. "What am I looking at?"

"These are my kids," I pointed to them one by one. "This is Amber, August, and Emily." I showed him the cat. I found a video on my phone of the kids singing happy birthday to Stanley. "Oh, look, this is a video," I said, and pressed play.

His mouth opened and he stared in shock at my device. He looked from the phone to me then back at the phone.

"You're serious?" he asked in a whisper. "You're

really from the future?"

"Yes," I said. "I'm from 2024."

"Okay, if you're from the future, tell me what's going to happen next year," he said in a testing tone.

"Okay, in the future, we won't be all that interested in history, apparently," I said. "At least I wasn't. I failed history in school. Speaking of schools, we have massive schools where each grade has its own room."

I showed him more videos. The kids' school Christmas concert. The kids singing in church when they were younger.

"Oh look!" I flipped to a picture of our car in our driveway. Unfortunately, Neil was in the picture. He'd been the one to insist I take a picture of *his* new car. "That's our car. Remember when I first asked you to call a taxi for me? I meant to call on a phone. And a taxi is a car like this one, but it's public transportation."

Cramming the entire future into one conversation was impossible.

"Oh wait," I said, flipping through my images as fast as I could. "I have a picture of planes at an airport." He sat silently with a persistent look of shock on his face. His jaw dropped when I showed him the pictures of the planes on the tarmac and some taking off that we'd taken from the airport windows when Neil had gone on a business trip.

"Airplanes," I explained. "Are like buses, or trains! But they fly in the sky. Really high. And really fast. They can carry hundreds of people at one time. In my time, it only takes five hours to travel by airplane from New York to California."

His jaw dropped lower, and he just stared at me

with his mouth hanging open. "My battery in my phone is really low," I told him. "I'll show you how I charge it."

He was silent as I pulled my solar power bank out of my purse. "This is a battery that is charged by the sun," I explained. "It stores the energy and then I can use it to charge my phone. See up here where it says my phone has only 10%?" I plugged in the cord from the solar power bank. "Now watch." After a few seconds, the 10% changed to 11%.

He just stared at me. "I'm sorry," I said. "Are you in shock? Do you need more proof? I do have one more thing that might prove it to you."

I pulled my driver's license out of my purse and held it out in front of him. "Look at my birthdate," I said.

He was stunned, and I was afraid I'd sent him into some kind of shock.

"I know it's a lot to take in," I said. "I'm sorry, but that's why I hadn't wanted to tell you. And that's why I want to go home. I miss my kids."

"What happened to your husband?" he asked in a whisper.

"That is another long story," I said. "I would prefer not to talk about him, if that's okay."

"Sure, sure," he nodded vigorously. "How . . . how are you going to get home? How did you get here?"

"I honestly am not sure," I said. "My uncle invited me over to his house to see his invention, which looking back, I'm thinking was a time machine. While waiting for him to get home, I discovered this thing, pressed a bunch of random buttons, and the next thing I knew, I was waking up in a field, and you and your friends were riding along."

"Oh," he said slowly as it dawned on him. "I thought you were in some kind shock or something because you kept asking if I was going to a parade!"

"Well, I thought you were," I said. "I had no idea I'd traveled through time. I thought it was still 2024 and that I had somehow blown up my uncle's house and car. Then when I noticed all his neighbors' houses were gone, and the telephone poles, it dawned on me something really weird had happened."

"Telephone poles?" he asked. I could see the confusion all over his face.

"Tall poles that the phone companies put in all along every road to every house and everyone in the world almost has a phone. Most people have cell phones like this that they carry with them and can call anyone at any time."

"Call someone," he said, pointing at my phone.

"Well, I can't," I said. "There would be no one to call. There aren't that many phones here in this time period. There are none like this."

He nodded slowly and seemed to remember his coffee. He took a slow sip.

"So, please," I said. "Please don't tell anyone about this, okay?"

"Of course," he said. "Wow!"

"I've been trying to assimilate to this way of life, but as you've noticed, it's not going very well," I admitted.

"If you need anything, just ask," he said. "My house is gonna be right on the other side of those trees."

"You know, I have an idea," I said slowly, trying to thoroughly think it through after I'd already begun the suggestion. "Since you have to drive so far every day to come out here just to work on building your house, what if you were to rent my loft? My job at the post office is going to be only for one more week, and I have no source of income here. You're paying $2 a night at the hotel, which will add up pretty quickly if you have to stay there the entire time until your house is built. That's $14 a week," I said. "If you were to rent my loft for, let's say, $5 per week, you would save a lot of money, and I would make some money."

He tilted his head sideways, and I could tell he was giving it careful thought.

"But what would the townsfolk say?" he asked, narrowing his eyes.

"You strike me as someone who doesn't really care all that much about what other people think," I told him.

"Oh, not about *me!*" he said. "*You!* I don't know what it's like in 2024, but here in 1884, it just ain't right for a woman to live with a man unless she's married to him."

"Are you trying to propose to me again?" I asked, eyeing him closely, but I smiled so he knew I was half-joking.

He laughed. "No, ma'am," he said. "I'm not stupid enough to propose to someone who's gonna be going far into the future at any given moment! But people in town *will* talk."

"Well, in 2024, I didn't care what other people thought, so I doubt I will care that much here," I said.

"There'll be gossip," he warned.

"You should see the gossip in the future!" I said.

"Imagine what it would be like if everyone that liked to gossip could call anyone they wanted and gossip from the comfort of their own home! All while laundry, cooking, and sweeping were done by machines."

He thought about it. "I really want to hear more about this future," he said solemnly. "But if you're sure."

"I am sure," I said. "To be honest, I *know* how to milk the cow, but still don't know the first thing about cows, or animals in general. If people say anything, you can tell them you're my farm hand."

He nodded. "$5 a week?" he asked, and I nodded. "It's a deal," he said, reaching across the table to shake my hand. "I'll get the rest of my things from the hotel tonight and settle up with Annie, and then I'll be back here in the morning."

He finished his coffee, rinsed his coffee cup at the sink, and then set it on the end of the table. "Do you need anything before I leave?" he headed to the door.

"I just need to know a couple of things first," I said. "Without a fridge, how do you keep milk from going bad? And also, how much does it cost to buy a horse and wagon?"

"You can rent a horse for 50 cents a day from the livery stable in town," he said. "A buggy will be an extra 50 cents a day."

"Seriously?" I asked in surprise. "I can just rent one?"

"Better than buying if you're not gonna be around here that long," he said. "A horse alone will cost you about $200 and a cheap wagon is somewhere around $60."

"That much?" I asked. "I figured they would be

dirt cheap."

"Transportation is expensive," he confirmed. "Most folks will get a mule or raise their own horses if they can."

"So, I hate to sound stupid," I said. "Keep in mind that I'm not from this century; what is a livery stable?"

"A place where you can rent a horse and buggy," he said with a smile. "Come on, I'll drive you into town."

I had only $1.49 left. I hoped I wouldn't be expected to pay in advance!

Chapter 14

Sunday was spent sewing together the edges of two six-foot lengths of bleached cotton by hand. For my $1.49, I'd been able to buy six yards of bleached cotton and some scissors, threads and needles, and still had some change. I figured I would make my own mattress so I could return Annie's to her. Carter knew a guy I could buy wool from to stuff it with, so I finally had my mattress dilemma solved.

As I stitched at the table, I thought about how much time it was taking, and back in 2024, I didn't seem to have the time to make anything, even with the sewing machine that I'd bought ten years before that had only been out of the box twice! Without a TV or internet to waste my time, I had plenty of time to sew and read. I felt like I was actually somehow improving myself and found myself more relaxed than I'd been in years.

With the lack of prepared foods in the store, and not much that I recognized at all, it turned out that I hadn't actually bought anything substantial for a meal. When Carter showed up at dusk, he was disappointed to find that I hadn't prepared a hearty meal for him.

I tried to hide my embarrassment, and finally had to confess my ineptitude. "I'm sorry, Carter, even back home, I wasn't much of a cook," I said dismally. "I don't know how to cook with these . . . ingredients." And I used the term *ingredients* loosely!

"Well, you have flour, sugar, butter," he said. He checked the bucket of milk that sat in the sink of cold water from the pump. I had been changing it frequently to keep it cold, but the cow was producing more than I could use in my coffee. "It's almost time to milk Bessie again, why don't I take this bucket over to the Henderson's farm and see if they can trade me for a few eggs?"

"Okay," I agreed quickly, gathering up the material from the table and throwing it on my bed.

"It's just down the road a ways, and I'll have to walk or else there won't be much left in the bucket after a wagon ride." He grabbed his jacket and hat, along with the bucket of milk and set off. In an hour, he returned with four eggs, $1 for me, and three half-grown chickens. "They have seven kids so can't really spare any more eggs," he explained. "But they're willing to buy the milk from you for five cents a gallon."

I almost balked at the insulting offer, but then realized that for five cents, I could buy quite a bit. And that would be five cents *a day* I'd be getting from the milk.

"Bessie produces about two gallons a day," he mused, putting some lard in the frying pan.

"I didn't buy lard," I said in surprise.

"I had some," he said. "In good weather I usually just camp out. I have some stuff. When the weather gets warmer, I'll be camping out on my own land while I finish my house."

"Oh," I said. "The cow's name is Bessie?"

"It is now," he said. "She didn't have a name, so I named her."

"Okay, fine," I said. "I don't use that much in my

coffee, so I could sell the whole two gallons a day to them."

"You'll need to keep some to make butter and for cooking," he said.

"Oh," I said. "Okay, well I think a half-gallon a day will be plenty for me. Speaking of which, I better get outside and pay Bessie a visit!"

I washed the bucket out thoroughly with boiling water and a soapy piece of linen and carried a clean, hot soapy cloth with me from the house out to see Bessie.

She walked right to me as soon as she heard me come out of the house. It wasn't fully dark yet, and the dim lantern light through the window allowed me enough light to milk by. I leaned my forehead against Bessie's side. She was warm and dusty.

"Tomorrow, I will find or buy a brush to spruce you up a bit," I told her as I washed her udder and began milking.

I rambled on to Bessie about how I missed my kids while I milked her. She stood quietly and seemed relaxed. When I finished, I washed her off again and gave her a warm pat. "You know, Bessie, you're better than my therapist. Not only are you free, but you're helping to support me. Thank you for the milk, Bessie." I gave her a one-armed hug around her neck before I left. As if she knew how inept I was, she walked herself back in the direction of the open-doored barn while I headed to the house.

"What do you feed chickens?" I asked Carter when I came inside. The little house was warm and smelled of flapjacks and fried beans.

"They eat worms from the ground," he said,

scooping the food onto the plates. "They'll eat eggshells, corn, whatever you feed them. Eating eggshells helps them make their own eggs have sturdier shells."

"How can that be true?" I asked. It didn't make sense to me. I reached for my phone, but realized there was no internet to settle this question for me. I had to take Carter's word.

Dinner was delicious, and I told Carter so. He just grinned and nodded and ate.

"Did you get much done on the house today?" I asked, trying to make conversation.

"Some," he said. He finished quickly and grabbed his hat and jacket. "I'll go unhitch the horses and feed the animals."

I wondered why his usually present grin was gone. He seemed serious for some reason and although I didn't dare to pry into his personal life, I wondered if was something I'd said. *Was he just annoyed because I hadn't prepared dinner?*

I'd learned from being with Neil not to let his moods affect mine. Whatever Carter had going on in his life really wasn't my business. I mused on this while I filled the sink from the kettle and washed the dishes. I had no drying rack, so I just piled them all in the frying pan on the counter beside the sink. I cut a one-foot section off of the bleached linen, then cut the width in half, ending up with two 16-inch by 12-inch dishtowels. I dried the dishes and set them carefully on the shelves above the sink. The frying pan, once dried to the best of my ability, went back on the back of the stove.

When Carter came in, he carried a rolled woolen blanket and climbed the ladder to the loft.

I was unsure as to whether or not he was coming back down or going to sleep, so I didn't say anything. He was clearly mad at me. *What did I do wrong?*

I successfully lit the fireplace to provide more light and to take the chill out of the air. The physical and atmospheric warmth filled me with peace. I wondered if this was why pioneers had seldom gotten divorced. Even the moodiest of men could be tolerated with a warm fire and pleasant atmosphere.

I realized that back in my *real* life, I'd always envisioned "the olden days" as being black and white, because any pictures I'd ever seen of my parents' great-grandparents were in black and white, but now that I was here, in my own cozy little house, whenever I thought about the future and its stark white ceiling lights and fluorescent lights in bland offices, *that felt more black and white than 1884!*

It had been a full week and Uncle Charlie hadn't shown up to save me. I wondered if I would be stuck here forever. I didn't know if his machine had somehow stored the numbers I'd punched and he would be able to get himself here to this same time, or if I was destined to die before I would ever be born?

Chapter 15

On Monday, I proudly rode my very own rented buggy to town after milking Bessie and having a cup of coffee. Carter was out the door with a canteen full of cold water from the pump just as I was coming in with the milk.

"Oh, you can take your kettle if you need it for the day," I said. "I'm going to be in town all day."

"I'll just come back here and eat lunch when I'm hungry," he said.

I just nodded and let him go. *I need to learn to cook!* I told myself. *And I need utensils and actual ingredients!* How I wished for my travel mug, which I would've never let go of if I'd known I'd be thrust back in time.

The owner of the post office was waiting for me when I arrived. "I'm not late, am I?" I asked, hurrying behind the counter. "I had to feed the chickens and milk the cow." I realized as I spoke that he was probably thinking, *who doesn't?*

"No, no, not at all," he said. "I just wanted to give you the good news. Irene is retiring, and you can have the job here full time if you like."

"What? That's fantastic!" I exclaimed. "Irene is okay, isn't she?"

"Yes, she's fine," he said. "She was mainly doing

it to keep busy, what with her husband gone and everything. But now her son and his family have come home, and she wants to spend as much time with her grandchildren as she can. She's fine, don't worry."

"Oh, I'm so glad for her!" I said. "She must be so happy to see her son!" I thought about August and how I'd give anything to see him right now, even with his occasional bratty attitude. I regretted giving him such a hard time about bedtime the last night I'd been there.

"Are you having second thoughts?" he asked, looking worried.

"Oh, no!" I said quickly, realizing my thoughts of August had automatically created a frown on my face. "I would be very happy to have this job! Thank you so much!"

"You're doing a great job here," he said. "Not that Irene didn't, mind you, but I did get some complaints that sometimes envelopes were not properly sealed."

I had no idea what he meant. I raised my eyebrows.

"It appeared to some people that they weren't the only ones reading their letters," he said carefully.

"Oh," I said slowly. "What? Really? Post office people do that?"

"Not supposed to!" he said.

"Well, thank you for the job!" I said. I was happy that I wasn't taking something from someone else.

I was so ecstatic over my permanent position, that I found myself humming while I sorted the morning mail after several people showed up with letters to mail at once.

At lunchtime, I sat outside the post office on a

bench and ate an apple I'd brought. Apparently there was no store-bought bread here. I wondered if I could buy bread from someone. I decided to take a stroll to see Annie and tell her about my job, but just as I stood, Daniel called to me.

"Taylor!" he shouted, hurrying towards me. "Are you heading to lunch?"

I showed him my apple. "Until payday, I think I'll be living on apples for lunch."

"What? No, come, let me buy you lunch," he offered. "An apple isn't much of a lunch."

"No, that's okay," I said. "You can't afford that!" I figured if teachers' salaries were similar in 1884 to 2024, I knew their wages were low.

"I can afford it, I promise," he said.

"But the hotel, the restaurant, it all adds up," I said.

"Oh, I'm not at the hotel anymore," he said. "Sorry, I thought you heard. I'm in the house next to the school now."

"Still, rent, or mortgage," I said.

He grinned and shook his brown hair out of his eyes. "The house for the teacher is free," he told me. He pointed to a cute white little cottage beside the school that was clearly visible from the side steps of the post office. "The teachers get a free house beside the school because the town wants to make sure even in the winters, I can get there. It's incentive to keep me here."

"Well, that's great," I said.

"So, come on, let me buy you lunch," he urged. "Please, I can afford it, besides, you know I don't like to eat alone."

I trusted his judgement, and I was hungry. "Just let me grab my bag," I said, running quickly into the post office. I didn't dare leave it laying around in case anyone broke in and saw my futuristic gadgets. I grabbed the key and locked the door, hoisted my bag over my shoulder and held my yellow calico dress high enough to keep it from dragging in the dirt, but not so high that my sneakers were noticeable.

Over a lunch of sandwiches and coffee (I'd learned on day one that I did not like tea), I shared my good news about my job with Daniel.

"That is great! Congratulations!" he said.

"You're not wearing your glasses!" I exclaimed, finally able to pinpoint why he looked so different today!

"I only wear them for reading," he said. "Which is most of the time, so it's rare that anyone sees me without them."

Not that he was unattractive with his glasses on, but without them it was easier to notice how Hollywood-gorgeous he was. I instantly felt so shallow. Besides his looks, Daniel was a nice, mild-mannered reliable man. And he was smart and polite. As I ate, I found myself accidentally comparing him to Carter who was somewhat rough around the edges. And then I found myself comparing them on purpose because I realized that I was getting far too attached to Carter. Daniel was clearly more suitable for me.

I was shocked by *that* thought. *I'm married and going back to the future soon!* I reminded myself. I was even more alarmed by the awareness that somehow, I'd placed myself in the exact same situation I'd been in when I was younger. Choosing between a smart-choice, mild-mannered and intelligent gentleman, and a bad-boy type, rough around the edges with a magnetic charisma that somehow held me emotionally captive.

"Is everything okay?" Daniel asked, and I realized I'd been silent for a while. "What's going on in that pretty little head of yours?"

"It's nothing," I said, shoving the last of my sandwich into my mouth so I wouldn't be expected to speak.

"Well, just remember," he said, reaching across the table and patting my hand. "I'm here if you ever need anyone to talk to."

"Thanks," I said. For a second, his hand rested on mine, and I didn't pull away. It felt nice, comforting, and warm. I couldn't remember the last time Neil had even looked at me, much less touched me.

For just that second, I allowed myself to indulge in the possibility of what my life would be like here if I never got to go home again. Obviously, I wouldn't want to be alone forever. I would end up marrying *someone* eventually, I was sure. It wasn't like I had the ability to go into the future and make sure my divorce from a cheating husband was final. And, technically, if I had no marriages on record prior to 1884, legally, in 1884, I wasn't married.

But I knew in my heart that I *was*. No timeline could erase the commitment I'd made to Neil and to my family. The very least I could do was make sure my divorce was final before feeling anything for anyone. No matter how smart, or charming, or handsome he might be.

"Well, I must get back to the school," Daniel said, checking his pocket watch. "I'll walk you back to the post office."

Chapter 16

Several weeks later, April arrived, and with it, a new resolve. It was clear I was never going to get back to my life in the future, so I had to make the best of it. I wasn't going to waste my life being miserable about something that was beyond my control. Every night before bed, I prayed for my children, that they would be safe, and that Neil would raise them well. Then I would cry myself to sleep, only to resolve the next morning to make the best of where I was and not dwell on the future.

With my full-time job plus the milk money, I was able to acquire all I needed for the house, bit by bit. A butter churn proved invaluable for making my own butter, which came with a learning curve. The churn was also good for storing milk overnight, sitting in a galvanized tub of cold water from the pump. The same tub that I was forced to have a bath in by lugging hot water from the water tank attached to the woodstove and then adding cold buckets of water from the pump. Carter thought it outrageous for me to have a bath more than once a week. After the first few baths, which were such a chore to prepare and then empty bucket-by-bucket, I came to agree with him. I soon became aware that my ways of the future wouldn't always work here.

I'd bought some wool from a sheep farmer and used it to fill the mattress I'd made. Annie was happy when she got her hotel mattress back. I was proud of my work, and if I was going to be stuck here forever, I decided I would learn how to make everything. I had so much wool, because I didn't know how much I would need, and I was unaware of how far my money would go, and I ended up making a mattress for Carter's bed in the loft. Plus, I made a third one for my bed, because I wasn't used to the 19th century level of discomfort that others apparently took for granted. I wanted to make my own dresses, maybe with a touch of future designs.

Carter and I quickly fell into an agreeable routine. I learned to cook breakfast, and he did the barn chores since he was used to getting up at 5 a.m.. By the time he was done everything at seven, breakfast was ready with filtered coffee, which he never failed to tell me was flavorless. His method of just dumping beans into a pot and boiling them, letting the coffee all settle to the bottom and then pouring was not for me. It was very bitter, even with the sugar and cream. I invested in my own kettle, and he was free to resume coffee-making that suited him, and I could enjoy the filtered coffee that was still stronger than I was used to.

In the evenings, I would read or sew by the fire, and he would whittle spoons and ladles for me. It was comfortable. I was at peace for those few hours before bed.

The first Friday in April was a stormy one, and by the time I left the post office to head home, the roads were nothing but mud, making the trek difficult. I had to go slowly and was properly soaked by the time I got home.

Carter was a pleasant sight when I reached my

yard. He ran out of the barn in the rain, held out a hand to help me out of the buggy, and then deftly unhitched the horse and took her into the barn. I hurried into the house but then realized that I'd left my purse in the buggy, so I hurried back out. The wind and rain were even stronger. I wished I'd had the forethought to park a little closer to the house. The ground was even muddier, and my sneakers sank up to my ankles. Because I was hurrying and my body was moving in a forward motion, once my sneakers got stuck, I went flying forward, flying out of my shoes and landing in the mud.

As I struggled to get to my feet, I heard Carter's roar of laughter. I couldn't get a footing in the soupy mud. "Hang on!" he called.

He hurried towards me, carefully picking higher spots of ground. "Are you hurt?" he asked.

"Just my pride," I said. "And not even that much because at least I don't live in the age of social media!"

"I have no idea what you're talking about," he said, reaching down to help me to my feet.

We were both soaked to the skin and my dress and hands were covered in mud. He pulled me to my feet but didn't let go of my hands right away. Instead, as the cold rain poured down upon us, he just stared into my eyes with a hint of a smile. It was as though time stood still, and for some reason my heart was pounding so loudly that I was sure he could hear it.

His eyes moved over my face and settled on my lips for a moment before moving back up to my eyes, as though he were searching for my soul.

Despite whatever my future past had held, I was here now, practically in his arms and I could no longer deny that I wished he would kiss me. But he didn't. He just took a deep breath, swallowed hard, and then let his breath out in one long sigh. He cleared his throat and shook his head slightly, as though he were shaking himself out of whatever insanity had put the idea of kissing me in his mind. And then he let my hands go slowly and stepped back barely an inch. "We should get in the house!" he said, looking up at the sky as though he had just noticed now that it was raining.

"Yes!" I agreed and turned, grabbing my sneakers out of the mud, my feet sinking back in. With effort I pulled my shoes free, only to be sent backwards into the mud again.

Carter turned, shook his head and rolled his eyes. "Lady, what *am* I gonna do with you?"

He bent down and picked me up as I clutched my sneakers. He was strong. Building his house and all the physical work had made him muscular. He carried me into the house as if I were light as a feather. I wondered if *he* thought I was getting "hippy". I was pleased that I'd actually lost weight since I'd been here. I didn't have a scale, but I could tell.

"Now," he said, setting me down on my feet just inside the door. "That one's free!"

I looked at him and he grinned. "The next time I carry a lady over the threshold, she'll be my wife!"

I grinned. *Would that be so bad?* I was soaked to the skin, covered in mud, my hair was soaked and muddy. "I need a bath!"

"This time, I can see it," he said. "I have to go back out and finish with the animals, but when I get back, I won't peek."

116

I carried the big metal washtub into my bedroom behind the fireplace and made several trips filling it with hot water from the stove. Then added a bucket of cold water to make it not scalding. I closed the cotton curtains we'd hung on either side of the fireplace so I could have privacy. Despite the tub being so small that I had to sit with my knees bent up almost to my chin, it was wonderful!

I bathed as quickly as I could, but still didn't make it out of the tub before Carter came back in the house.

"I'm not peeking!" he called. "And I got your purse from the buggy!" I heard him chopping vegetables on the sideboard, as he called it. I referred to the wooden table that contained the pump and sink, a counter, but eventually went with his name for it. I didn't want to sound weird if somehow it was referenced in conversations I had with other women in the town. Apparently everyone just called it a sideboard.

"What are we having?" I called as I got out of the tub and dried off quickly with a bath towel I'd made.

"Pheasant stew!" he yelled.

"Pheasant?" I asked in surprise. *Isn't pheasant a luxury food?* I wondered.

"Pheasant *stew!*" he replied.

I quickly dressed in my jeans and T-shirt. I hated that I only had one outfit from the future, and laundry was not something I had the energy or time to do more than once a week.

By the time I emptied the tub, put my muddy clothes into it, and cleaned up all the mud from the kitchen floor, the stew was almost ready.

"I miss how easy things were in the future," I pouted.

"Stew's almost ready," Carter said, stirring the pot.

"It smells delicious!" I said. "I've never had pheasant stew!"

"Really?"

"Really."

"What, are pheasants extinct in the future?" he asked, looking genuinely concerned about the future of pheasants.

"No, just really expensive," I said.

"Huh," he said thoughtfully. "Maybe I oughta start farming pheasants then."

"Where did you get this one?"

"Henderson shot a bunch this morning," he said. "Oh, by the way, speaking of the Henderson's, we can't sell them milk anymore."

"What?" I asked. "I was counting on that money! Did they buy their own cow or something?"

"No, nothing like that," he said. "But Bessie's pregnant. She's probably gonna calf in a month or two and we have to let her rest. You don't milk this close to calving."

"Oh," I said. "He sold me a *pregnant* cow?"

"Actually," Carter turned and looked at me with a wide grin. "He sold you two for the price of one. But that's why he said the cow wouldn't make it out west. He didn't want to slow down for calving."

Shortly after a delicious dinner, and once I'd done the dishes, we turned in. It had been a long, arduous day.

As tired as I was, I couldn't fall asleep. When

thunder rumbled and crackled overhead, and the beating of the rain intensified on the roof, it reminded me of the last time I'd spent the night consoling Emily during a thunderstorm. That reminded me of home, and I soon found myself scrolling through my pictures on my phone again. I'd accepted the fact that I would be forced to live the rest of my life here now, but that didn't make the pain of losing my children any easier. My heart ached to see them laugh, to hug them and hold them. I couldn't hold back the tears, and I didn't turn my phone off until I couldn't contain the sobs that were stuck in my throat. I rolled over and sobbed into my pillow. I knew Carter would never hear me between his snoring, the pounding rain on the roof, and the raging thunder overhead.

I sobbed for at least fifteen minutes before my privacy curtain was pulled aside and Carter was there.

"Are you okay?" he asked.

"I just miss my kids so much!" I admitted.

He turned and left without saying a word. *He probably thinks I'm weak,* I thought. *Who cares? He has no idea what it's like to be torn away from your children!*

I heard him banging around with pots and pans in the kitchen. *Figures, a woman is in the middle of a nervous breakdown and all the man can think about is his stomach.* These thoughts ran rampant through my mind until I realized that I shouldn't be expecting anything from him anyway. It wasn't like he was my husband. He was a boarder, for heaven's sake! *Get a grip, Taylor!*

I heard him climb back up the ladder to his loft. I didn't care. I sat up in bed and reached for one of the little cotton handkerchiefs I'd made after Mr. Bell at the mercantile looked at me like I'd lost my mind when I asked him if he had any tissues. I'd ended up buying a pack of handkerchiefs that day but got much more satisfaction out of making my own, given how much I cried over my children each night.

"Can I come in?" Carter asked, whipping my privacy curtain aside again.

I nodded. "I thought you went back to bed," I said.

"I had to get some pots to put up there," he said. "Did you know your roof leaks?"

"No," I said, wiping my tears with my handkerchief.

"Yeah, in three spots," he said. "But anyway, what's wrong?"

"I'm never going to be able to go back home," I said with fresh tears springing to my eyes.

His head tilted sideways slightly and in the dim light from the fireplace that was still giving us warmth in the storm, he sat down on the edge of my bed and pulled me into his arms.

"I'm sorry," he whispered, stroking my hair gently. I felt him softly kiss my hair.

When my tears were exhausted, he gently lay me down and looked into my eyes, his face was inches from mine. My heart started pounding in my ears again. *Is he going to kiss me?*

"You need to get some sleep," he whispered. "I'll be right upstairs if you need me."

I need you now! I screamed in my mind but didn't dare to say it out loud. Instead, I just nodded.

"Goodnight," he whispered and gave me a soft kiss on the forehead. "Try to get some sleep."

120

Chapter 17

On Monday, after a tense weekend of trying to figure out how it would work if I *did* want to marry Carter—while I scrubbed clothes by hand on a washboard—I was thankful to have the easy job of just managing the town's mail.

It was a slow mail day, so instead of reading, I indulged in daydreaming about what my future would look like if I married Carter. I imagined we would have a bunch of kids. Birth control didn't seem to exist here; every family seemed to have a bunch of kids. I wondered if raising kids would be easier without all the technology and video games. There were always kids out playing, climbing trees, running around. And they were polite to adults!

At lunchtime I had lunch with Daniel as usual. He looked especially nice today, wearing a suit.

"What's the occasion?" I asked over our sandwiches. "Is there a new dress code for teachers?"

"My girlfriend is arriving with my parents this afternoon," he said, nearly bursting at the seams with joy.

"Oh, your *girlfriend* is arriving today!" I said, trying to sound like I was genuinely thrilled for him.

"We are engaged to be married," he said with a wide smile. "Mary is coming in today on the two-o'clock train."

"Well, congratulations," I told him. *Boy, did I ever read his signals wrong!* I'd thought he had some kind of feelings for me but was just shy. If he did indeed have feelings for me, he'd never intended to act on them. I tried to ignore the petty jealousy I felt.

However, the petty jealousy I'd felt at the discovery of Mary paled in comparison to the real jealousy I felt when a letter came in from the train that afternoon for Carter! It was written with female handwriting and the return address told me from it was a woman named Charlotte Martin in California! I flipped it over and she'd written *XOXO* on the back and drew a little heart. Her drawing wasn't that good, if you ask me; the heart was all crooked and the bottom lines crossed over way too far.

I stewed over the letter until closing time. I debated ignoring it and just giving it to him if he came into town to check his mail. But that felt too mean. I knew I would take it to him. It was the right thing to do. I was so furious for allowing myself to fall for him! Sure, I had a husband, but he was 140 years in the future! And was soon to be my ex-husband! It wasn't like I had any expectations of ever seeing him again! I had foolishly allowed myself to indulge in romantic feelings towards someone else. I could almost justify that to myself, but I couldn't justify *him* making me fall in love with him when he knew very well he already had a woman waiting for him in California! Although, granted, he hadn't really done anything. *Maybe that's why he stopped himself from kissing me over the weekend!* It all made sense now. Was Charlotte now going to show up on a train the same way Daniel's girlfriend had?

It was clear to me that a woman had to stake her claim on a man fast in the 1800s before someone else scooped up his attentions. Now all of his behaviors had made sense. Why he'd hesitated before moving into my house with me. The "gossip" he'd probably been worried about was Charlotte hearing about him living in a house with another woman!

I put his letter in my purse, knowing that my anger was all at my *own* actions, not at Carter's. He'd actually been the perfect gentleman. It was *I* that had to learn not to overstep my boundaries with men. Although it would've been helpful if he'd mentioned Charlotte to me!

The last two hours of the day dragged on until finally, it was time to lock up and go home and give Carter his letter. I wondered how he would react when he realized I *knew*.

As I was locking the door, I heard Daniel call my name. "Wait up!" he said.

I locked the door and turned and there he was, hurrying from the school with a beautiful blonde lady on his arm. She looked to be no more than 20, if that.

"Taylor, I'd like you to meet my fiancée, Mary Baker," Daniel said proudly, grinning from ear to ear. "I'm taking her around to meet the town."

"Nice to meet you," I said to her. I honestly had no idea what to say after that. Social small talk was never something I'd excelled at.

"Mary, this is Taylor Cooper," he told her. "She's a relative newcomer too."

"*Taylor Cooper?*" Mary said in astonishment.

"I know, I know," I said, holding up my hand and

smiling. "It's an odd name for a girl, I've been told that."

"No, that's not it," Mary said, her blue eyes growing big and round. "It's just that I met this man at a train station that asked me if knew a woman named Taylor Cooper!"

"What?" I shrieked. "What did he look like? What train station?"

"The last stop before here," she said. "I don't remember what the name of the town was."

"The last stop before here is Weaver Settlement," Daniel added.

"What did he look like?" I asked. "Did you get his name? Was it Charlie?"

"Yes, it was Charlie," she said, looking proud that she'd been able to relay a message. "He said he was looking for his niece named Taylor Cooper, but I told him I'm from Oregon and don't know anyone around these parts."

"Okay, this was today?" I asked.

"Yes, about an hour ago," she said. "He was asking everyone on the platform if they'd seen you out west."

"I hope he's not heading there looking for me," I said. "I have to get to Weaver Settlement!"

"The next train going west is tomorrow morning," Daniel told me.

"Okay, thank you so much, Mary!" I gave her a hug, causing her to giggle and nearly lose her balance.

I hurried to my buggy and, after several confusing directions from locals, found the house of the man that owned the post office, whose name I still hadn't gotten.

124

"I have to be gone tomorrow," I told him as soon as he opened his door. "It's a family emergency!"

"Okay," he said. "Thank you for letting me know. Will you be back the next day?"

"To be honest, I'm not sure," I said. "But I will try to be!" I knew that if my uncle was here, that meant he'd created a device that would allow us to zap ourselves back home, but I couldn't say out loud that I might never be coming back to Harper Falls. This town had welcomed me in and treated me like one of its own. But also, I knew if I heard it out loud with my own ears, my heart would break a little. It had already been broken so much, there wasn't much left to break.

I hurried home, and yet it seemed to take forever. I was no longer jealous of Carter's letter. If I was leaving, he would need someone that would make him happy. He *deserved* someone with no past or future baggage. That person was *not* me.

When I got home, it was still early, and Carter hadn't returned from working on his house yet.

I got the clothes off the line that stretched from the corner of the house to a tree, propped up in the middle with a forked pole, which kept the line up so that the long dresses didn't drag in the dirt.

Once the clothes were all folded, I put a nightgown, along with my modern clothes, in a carpet bag that Annie had given me when I first moved. I rolled them so they wouldn't wrinkle. At least not as much, I hoped.

I put on my apron and made a meal of brown beans and beef and set about making bread, knowing it would be long after supper before it was ready to go into the oven. I figured Carter would appreciate having fresh bread in the house for a day or two after I was gone. While supper was being cooked, and bread was rising, I grabbed the straw broom and swept the floor, sweeping the dust out the door. And right into Carter!

He coughed, blinked hard, and went back outside, continuing to cough.

"I'm so sorry!" I said. "Are you okay?"

"I will be," he said, still coughing. "Lady, you're gonna be the death of me!"

"Sorry," I said again.

He followed me into the house. "Wow, something sure smells good!" he said. "And I'm starving!"

"It will be ready soon!" I said.

"And you're making bread!" he said in surprise. "So, is this your way of saying you'll agree to be my wife?"

"No," I said, smiling and rolling my eyes. "It's—"

"Hold that thought!" he said, putting a finger up to my lips. "I brought you something!"

"You did?" I asked.

He ran back out the door and then returned a minute later with a brown package.

"What is it?" I asked, looking at his face for clues. "It's too big to be an engagement ring!"

"Open it," he said, smiling.

"It's not my birthday," I said.

"Well, it's kinda like our anniversary since we've been living together now a whole month," he said.

"Really? Has it been that long?"

"Time flies when you're having fun!" he said. "Now open it!"

126

"Okay, okay," I said, pulling off the string and opening the brown paper. "Shoes!"

They were shoes with heels and buttons up the sides. They came with a shoe hook inside to do up the buttons.

"Why did you do this?" I asked in surprise.

"Because I wanted to," he said. "Now try them on."

I sat on the bench and kicked off my sneakers that had become so uncomfortable after being ruined by the mud. I pulled on one of the new shoes and Carter took the shoe hook and showed me how to button up the sides of them.

"They fit perfectly!" I said, looking at him in amazement. "How did you know what size shoe to get?"

"I measured your feet while you were sleeping," he said, laughing.

"No, you didn't!" I said. "I would've felt it!"

"Ah, you were just snoring away," he said. He laughed a good hearty laugh and then grabbed one of the wooden spoons he'd made and stirred the beans and beef. "Looks like supper's ready!"

"Thank you for the shoes," I said. "But I didn't get you anything."

"Just being here is enough," he said. "When a man gets to come home to a clean house, a beautiful woman, and the smell of a good dinner and fresh bread, what more could he ask for?"

It was that moment that convinced me that we had *something*. I didn't know what that something was, but it was definitely something. A cozy home and a relationship that I didn't want to lose. Not to Charlotte and not to the future with Neil. The memory of Charlotte dampened my happiness, and I remembered the letter.

"Oh, I *do* have something for you after all!" I said, pretending to be happy about it. "A letter came for you today!"

"A letter?" he asked in surprise, scooping out food into the plates. "Now, who would wanna write me a letter? Is it from you?"

"No, silly," I said, grabbing the letter from my purse and handing it to him.

He took it and I watched the smile on his face fade as he read the address and turned it over. "Well, I'll read it later," he said, but his smiles and laughter had turned to deep lines on his forehead, and we struggled to make conversation as we ate.

Chapter 18

Once Carter had retreated to the loft with his letter, I cleaned the kitchen and felt empty. I put the bread in the oven and sewed some pillows by the fire. I had wool left and empty time while waiting for the bread. I'd already made pillows for me and Carter, but I wanted a second one, and he probably would too. By the time the bread was out of the oven, tapped out of the pans onto a linen towel on the table and smothered in butter all over the tops, I had only to fill the pillowcase and stitch the opening shut.

I filled the pillow, stitched it, threw it on my bed, wrapped the still-warm bread in linen, and then took a final trip out to the outhouse for the evening. That was one part of 1884 I was *not* going to miss! Before I found out Uncle Charlie had found me, *almost found me*, I had already been rolling around ideas in my head of how to build a flushing toilet. In the winter, I was *not* going to be traipsing outside to go to an outhouse and that was that!

By the time I fell into bed, exhausted, I realized that I'd forgotten to tell Carter that I was leaving the following morning. I could hear him snoring, and I wasn't going to wake him with that news. Besides, the fact that he'd disappeared immediately after supper told me all I needed to know. He was in love with some girl named Charlotte, and she'd likely be arriving shortly after I left.

The thought of another woman in *my* house irked me, but I'd already let him work his way in. It had already been a home to both of us. Now I'd be leaving.

The thought of leaving permanently ate at me. I didn't *want* to leave permanently. Sure, I wanted to go back to the future, for my kids, but I'd found that this slower pace of life had been what I'd needed all along. I could see a million stars in the sky at night. Even the house was quiet. I mean actually *quiet!* No humming of the fridge, blaring of TVs. I'd never even noticed but just the background inaudible hum of all the electric appliances and computers and electricity had somehow been noise that had gone unnoticed. Until it was removed. Now, the silence was actually *completely* silent.

I lay awake into the early hours of the morning working out a new plan. I would be going to the future all right, but it wouldn't be forever. I would go and get my children and bring them back here! This was what *they* needed too! Sure, it would be a bit of a culture shock, more so for August and Amber, but it would be a better life for them.

My plan was hatched. Even without Carter in my life, I knew I wanted this life, this house that in just a month I'd been able to turn into a cozy home. If Uncle Charlie hadn't shown up, I'd planned on braiding a rug to go by the fireplace. I would learn how to spin wool into yarn. I would build indoor plumbing. When I got to the future, I would buy every single eBook on homesteading, pioneer life, how to install indoor plumbing, and whatever else I could think of. I would also bring back modern medicines. Who knew when we would need it. With this new plan, I was too excited to sleep!

When I awoke in the morning, Carter had already left. He'd clearly been put in an awkward position by receiving a letter from his girlfriend. When I thought about all the times he'd flirted with me, I became angry. *He knew* he had a girlfriend.

While I drank a strong cup of coffee, I wrote a note for Carter.

Dear Carter,

Thank you for all the help and kindness you've shown me. I must go away for a few days, but I will be back. Please look after Bessie for me.

Taylor

I debated putting *xoxo* after my name just for fun but decided against it. He had someone. I was happy for him. At least I tried to convince myself I was.

I grabbed my carpet bag and purse and checked the stove. Carter had lit it before I'd gotten up, so the fire was nearly out. Future habits had me feeling uneasy about leaving the house and leaving the stove "on".

I was thankful that Carter had hitched up my horse to the buggy before he'd left. *That was kind of him.*

I took in the beautiful countryside as I rode to town. I would miss this if I had to leave forever. Miss it more than I would miss the future century of stress and corporate politics. Besides, with all the information I could bring back with me from the future, I could learn how to build a washing machine. The one thing I would bring back for sure would be a heck of a lot more underwear!

When I reached town, I returned the horse and buggy and paid what I owed, then I went to see Annie and paid her the rest of what I owed her. At least in this time period, I'd been able to get debt-free. Other than the house and the cow.

"I'm glad you located your uncle," Annie said, but she looked wistful. "But I'm going to miss you!" She gave me a long hug.

"Don't worry," I said. "I'll be back. I love this town, my job, and my house. I will be back!"

"Is Carter going with you?" she asked.

"No, why?" I asked in surprise.

"Well, I thought you and he were together," she said. "I figured I'd be getting a wedding invitation any day the way he talks."

"Well, it's not me he's professing his love for," I told her. "He has a girlfriend from out west named Charlotte. She'll probably be coming here, or he'll be going there. He and I; no."

"Aw," she said with a frown. "I thought you two made such a great couple. You can't tell me you don't find him handsome."

"Oh, yes, he's handsome, alright," I admitted. "And to be honest, I may have even been starting to fall in love with him. But, like I said, he already has someone he's in love with. Probably engaged to. I'm not going to get between two people in love."

"He's never mentioned anyone," Annie said. "Are you sure?"

"Let's put it this way," I said, "I work in the post office and yesterday, a letter came for him from a woman named Charlotte, and she had hearts and hugs and kisses all over the back of the envelope. So, I'm pretty sure there's something there."

"Maybe the letter was a break-up letter," she said

hopefully.

"With Xs and Os?" I reminded her with a smile. "I don't think so."

"Well, next time I see him, I'm gonna give him a slap upside the head for you," Annie said.

"No need to do that," I said with a laugh. "He was with her before he met me, I have no claim on him."

"Well, there's plenty of cowboys out there," she said. "I'll keep my eyes open for one until you get back."

I laughed, we hugged again, and I left.

I was so focused on everything in the future that I could bring back with me, that I didn't begin to miss Carter until I was seated on the train. I lurched forward in my seat as the train pulled away from the platform, blowing its whistle. The racket, shaking, and thick black smoke billowing past my window as we rode came as a surprise, but my heart soared as I headed with hope towards the future!

I figured that once I found my uncle, we could instantly zap back to the future. I would spend a few days doing anything I needed to do to finalize my divorce, getting my kids oriented and packed, and gathering everything I would need for us to survive in the 19th century. I could imagine how annoyed the older kids might be about the transition, but I was sure this would be a good thing for them. They'd become little more than zombies with their attention constantly tied to electronic devices.

The train ride to Weaver Settlement only took an hour, and I scanned the platform for my uncle. I'd thought perhaps he'd been greeting every train in hopes of finding me. But there were only a few people on the platform, and most were waiting to get on.

I went up to the small ticket booth. "Excuse me, do you know of a Charlie Davis that was here in town recently?"

"Oh yes," the guy behind the counter said, adjusting his tiny round glasses. "He was searching for his niece."

"Okay, I'm his niece," I said. "Do you know if he's still here?"

"You can ask around town," he said.

"Okay, thanks," I said, even though he'd not been very helpful.

I hurried down the hill and went to the stagecoach station and asked. They remembered Uncle Charlie and thought he might still be in town but didn't know where.

Then I remembered my experience when I'd first landed in 1884. Carter had thought I was delusional and had taken me straight to the doctor! I went to find the doctor. I couldn't for the life of me remember his name, but I knew where to find him. I waited in the front room in a chair by the window until he came out of the back with his patient, an elderly lady who he walked all the way out to her carriage on his arm.

When she was safely in her carriage and on her way, he came back in and stared at me with his hands on his hips. "Well, well, well," he said with a wide smile. "I didn't think I'd be seeing you back here again. How have you been?"

"I've been doing well," I said. "How have you been doing? And how's Mary?" *At least I hope his wife's name is Mary,* I thought. I was so terrible with names.

"Oh, she's fine," he said.

"I'm looking for my uncle," I said. I was as terrible with small talk as I was with names. "His name is Charlie Davis, a short older guy, and he was probably confused and didn't know what year it is."

"There was a Charlie Davis here yesterday," he said. "But he wasn't confused. He seemed fine to me. He did ask me if I knew you, though."

"What did you tell him?" I asked.

"I told him you went to Harper Falls," he said. "And I told him there was a stagecoach leaving this morning."

"Oh no!" I said. "I just came from there to meet him here. Please don't tell me he took the morning stage!"

"No," he said with a chuckle. "He said he preferred the train and is planning on leaving on the afternoon train today."

"So, he's still here?" I asked in shock. "Still in town?"

The doctor nodded. "He stayed at the boarding house at the end of town for the night."

"Thanks so much!" I exclaimed and gave the doctor a hug. "You've been so helpful!"

I lifted my skirts, and awkwardly ran down the street. The weight of the carpet bag in my left hand and my purse over my right shoulder created an awkward balance, and I wasn't used to the new shoes Carter had given me. My sneakers had been ruined, and I was forced to wear the new shoes.

Thankfully, Weaver Settlement was much smaller than Harper Falls, although it hadn't been laid out as neatly. Still, the boarding house was easy to find. I hurried to the tall two-story building that looked like the outside of it had been scorched in a lightning storm. I knocked, and when there was no answer, I opened it and stepped inside.

A middle-aged woman in a grimy apron and carrying a bucket of gray water came around the corner. "Hello?" she called.

"Hi, I'm looking for a Charlie Davis," I said. "I understand he spent the night here. I'm his niece."

"Oh, Charlie," she said with an instant smile. "Yes, he's been here for a few days. He's still in his room this morning. Up in room 2 at the top of the stairs."

"Thanks!" I couldn't contain my excitement.

"You're just in time, too," the woman called after me. "He's catching the afternoon train!"

My mind raced as I hurried up the narrow steps with risers that were far too high. I wondered where we would have to go to be zapped back to the future. We obviously couldn't just leave in his room. That would be too suspicious if two people went into a room and never, ever came out. Not to mention where this exact location might be in the future. We would have to get back to the spot where Carter had found me.

I knocked on the door.

"Come in," he called, and I opened the door. *It was him!* He was facing away, putting some things into a suitcase.

"Uncle Charlie!" I shrieked, dropping my bag and purse by the door.

"Taylor!" he said, whipping around with a broad grin. "I've been looking for you!"

We hugged, and I was already beginning to feel like I was home again.

"Where have you been?" he asked.

"I was found on a trail, picked up by a cowboy and brought here to see the doctor because I was babbling about not believing I was in the year 1884," I said, looking back on it with a smile.

"Oh, Doctor Walker," Uncle Charlie said. "He's such a nice guy, isn't he?"

I nodded. "So, when can we leave?" I asked. "I can't wait to see my kids!"

"Now hold on," he held up his hands. "We can't go back yet."

"What?" I asked. "Why not?"

"Well, I don't exactly have the Back Zapper finished yet," he admitted.

"The Back Zapper?" I asked.

"It's like a key fob," he said. "I've been working on it ever since you disappeared. I'm designing it so that when a person travels through time, they can automatically be recalled using the Back Zapper."

"But it's not finished?" I asked. He shook his head. "How far away from being done are you?"

He shrugged. "Well, to be honest, I don't know," he admitted sheepishly. "But I have the design figured out and all of the parts, more or less. I brought everything I need with me so I can build it here."

He had three large suitcases laid out on his bed, along with a duffle bag. He pointed to each one. "Laptop, tablet, and supplies in this one. Solar panels, electronic parts, and chargers in that one. And last, but not least, rechargeable tools in that one."

"What's in the duffle bag?" I asked, not as interested as I was when I thought we were zapping out of here immediately.

"My clothes!" he said with a look of pure joy. "I went to a costume shop and bought all the 19th century clothing I could find! I found some of it at thrift shops and such."

"At least you were prepared to land here," I said. "I wish I'd been."

"Taylor, I told you to go in my house and wait for me," he said. "I didn't tell you to touch anything!"

"I know, I'm sorry," I said. I really did have only myself to blame. "I'm just saying, I wish I'd been prepared."

"Well, if it helps, I have a ton of 1880s money," he said. "Some even from the 1700s!"

"How?" I asked.

"I had my coin collection, and that had quite a lot of 19th century coins," he said. "But then I went online and bought up all I could find. I'm rich!"

"How much rich?" I asked skeptically.

"I have $5000!" he said. "It cost me a lot more than that, though. But I put it on my credit card and that's a future problem!"

"Why do I get the feeling that we aren't going home anytime soon?" I asked. "You said you have all you need to build the key fob thing."

"Don't worry, we'll go home," he assured me, patting my arm. "Just be patient! I figure if I invest in things in 1884, when I get back to the future, I'll be rich!"

"Okay," I said. "That doesn't sound too bad. But how long are you planning on staying in 1884?"

He shrugged and shook his head. "I don't know," he said. "I want to enjoy the scenery, see what life was really like. I've been thinking of joining the wagon train west that is stopping here in town in a few days. I've always wanted to go on an exciting adventure!"

"But Uncle Charlie!" I felt my heart sink. "You're not in any rush to go home?"

"Not at the moment," he said brightly, oblivious to my dilemma.

"But I haven't seen my kids for more than a month!" I said. "I have been crying myself to sleep every night! And if you go on a wagon train west, what about me?"

"Come with me," he said. "As soon as I build the zapper, you'll be able to go home, but I won't have to leave. Don't worry so much!"

"I don't think you understand how hard life is here," I said. "I've been living here for over a month. If you go west, it is not going to be an easy journey. You won't have time to even think about building your zapper!"

"Of course I will!" he insisted. "What else do you think I'll be doing while sitting on a wagon riding along behind a team of horses?" He laughed.

"I have a job and a house," I told him. "And a cow."

"You have a cow?" he asked.

"Yes, and a house, and a job at the post office in Harper Falls," I said. "If I'm not going to be able to go back to the future any time soon, I may as well go back to my house and my cow!"

"But if you don't come with me," he teased. "How will you be able to get the zapper when I finish it?"

He had me. I could feel my shoulders tense up. I forced my voice to be calm because getting into a heated argument with a man who just happened to be my lifeline, *literally*, was not a good idea. "Look, Uncle Charlie," I began slowly. "How about this; the wagon train doesn't leave for a few days, so since you've already booked a train ticket for this afternoon, come with me back to Harper Falls. You can meet my friends, see my house, and my cow. And my boarder."

"You have a boarder?" he asked in surprise. "Wow, you've really settled in here!"

"I didn't have much choice," I reminded him. "By the way, how did you figure out what year I was in?"

"When I got home, the panel was still flashing 140," he said. "So, I knew you'd traveled back 140 years. When I had all the materials I needed to bring, I came to rescue you. I knew I could build my Back Zapper here, but I didn't want you to be lost and alone in 1884. I got here as quick as I could!"

"Thanks," I said. "I do feel better now that you're here."

"Let's go grab a bite to eat and head to the train station!" he said. "And you can show me your house!"

Chapter 19

After we arrived in Harper Falls, I introduced Uncle Charlie to Annie, and Mabo. I showed him the post office where I worked. Uncle Charlie insisted on wiring the rest of the cost of the house and cow to Isaac so I could be free and clear of debt. When Isaac's brother at the bank handed me the official deed to the property with my name on it, I felt an overwhelming sense of belonging, like I had really become part of the community now. I owned a piece of Harper Falls. I was now part of 1884.

Then Uncle Charlie bought himself a covered wagon and four horses, and we went into Bell's General Mercantile.

"I'm heading west, and I'll pick up all the supplies tomorrow," he proudly said to Mr. Bell. "Here is a list of everything I need, but anything you think that I'll need that I didn't account for, please just throw it in as a nice surprise, okay?" He handed Mr. Bell a piece of paper, and Mr. Bell smiled.

As we were leaving, Daniel and Mary walked in, along with Daniel's parents. "Taylor!" Daniel said, smiling broadly. "This must be your uncle!"

"Yes," I said, glad that Uncle Charlie could meet even more of my friends. Maybe if he saw how I'd settled in here, he wouldn't be so anxious to take off out west before finishing his device. I introduced my uncle, and Daniel introduced us to his parents. For the first time in my life, I felt like I was having the grown-up *normal* life that I'd always dreamed about, just not in the correct century.

When Uncle Charlie was satisfied with his preparations, we headed out to the house in his newly acquired wagon. It was loud and bumpy as the iron wheels rumbled along the dirt road while the chains on the horse harness rattled and rang.

"A six-month trip out west is going to be a bumpy ride!" I told him.

"It won't sound as bad once it's full," he said.

"It will sound worse!" I insisted. "With all your stuff bouncing around!"

After all the time spent in town, the sun was already setting when we pulled into the yard. Right behind Carter!

"Hey, there!" Carter called, unhitching his horses. "I see you traded in your buggy for a wagon and a man!"

He came over and helped me down from the wagon, and I was proud of his manners. Uncle Charlie *had* to see the value of the life I'd already carved out for myself.

"Carter, this is my Uncle Charlie that I told you about," I said as Carter also helped Uncle Charlie down. "Uncle Charlie, this is Carter."

"Ah, the boarder!" Uncle Charlie said, reaching out and shaking Carter's hand. "Pleased to meet you!"

"Pleased to meet you too," Carter said. I thought I saw his smile fade when Uncle Charlie referred to him as the boarder, and not guest or friend. I cringed a little.

"Let me help with the animals," Uncle Charlie insisted.

"I'll go start supper," I said, anxious to leave them.

I was pleased to see that Carter hadn't found my note yet. I grabbed it from the table and used it to light a fire in the stove. I chopped up some salted beef and threw it into the pot, and peeled potatoes at the table. I was going to make the heartiest beef stew my uncle had ever tasted. He'd also get to see that I'd learned to bake bread because all the bread from the night before was still there. Even I had to admit that my homemade butter from the last of Bessie's milk was the best I'd ever tasted.

As I'd hoped and predicted, Uncle Charlie was impressed. So was Carter. I was happy in my cozy little house as Uncle Charlie informed Carter about all the inventions in the future. They discussed Hollywood and found out that Hollywood didn't even exist yet, much to Uncle Charlie's dismay because he'd had big plans of becoming a major player in Hollywood. Carter did nothing to try to change my uncle's mind about leaving. Perhaps if I mentioned that I'd have to leave too, he might've tried. But I didn't even want to voice that possibility. I had no intention of leaving! Especially now that my house was totally paid for. It was really *mine!*

When we were all full, Carter lit the fireplace, and we sat around and talked about the future and the present. Carter filled us in on how to do things in the present, and Uncle Charlie gave him dreams of possibilities in exchange.

"It's okay if my uncle rooms with you for the

night, isn't it?" I asked Carter. "I've made two mattresses for my bed, so one of you could sleep on the floor." I hated to ask it of Carter since he was paying me for the loft, but with just the loft and my tiny room, there really wasn't any other option.

"Fine by me," Carter said with a grin. "This way!"

"A ladder?" Uncle Charlie said, looking up. "You sleep up there? I'm afraid I can't climb ladders."

I felt a little wave of satisfaction that my uncle was becoming aware that he wasn't as fully prepared for this century as he'd thought. Maybe that would change his mind about embarking on such a massive adventure that was so unpredictable.

"Isn't there a place down here I can sleep?" Uncle Charlie asked, looking around. "I can sleep on the floor by the fire!"

"No, Uncle Charlie, you can't sleep on the floor!" I said.

"Then the barn," he suggested with an enthusiastic smile. "I'm okay in the barn."

"No," I insisted. "Okay, look, you can have my bed, and I can sleep on the floor by the fire."

"No way," Carter interjected. "He can have your bed, you can have my bed, and I'll sleep on the floor."

"There really isn't that much room between the fireplace and the table," I pointed out.

"I didn't say by the fire," Carter said with a grin. "You can have my bed, and I can sleep on the floor in the loft."

I looked at him and considered the effects of us sleeping in that limited proximity.

144

"Don't worry, princess, I won't bite," he said. "Heck, I'm used to camping out, a floor ain't no problem!"

"Great! It's settled then!" my uncle said, gleefully rubbing his hands together.

Carter on the floor less than three feet from my bed gave me both a sense of comfort and anxiety. After five minutes of silence, I rolled over on my side to face him. The full moon shed light into the loft, creating a surreal peace.

"Are you still awake?" I whispered.

"Mhm," he mumbled.

"Listen, do you think you could talk my uncle out of going west on this wagon train?" I asked. "I don't think he'll survive."

"From what he's said, I think he can handle it as well as the next guy," Carter said. "Besides, what would I say?"

"I don't know," I said. "Help him find a job, or a local adventure."

"But that's not what he wants," Carter whispered back. "He wants to go on a real adventure, and from what I've heard about the future, nobody seems to really be living all that much there."

He was right. In the future, I'd been sitting down all the time. Sitting down for eight hours a day at a stressful corporate job, then sitting down all evening watching TV or doing even more work. Or I was sitting in the car commuting to work or being the family taxi for the kids. I'd noticed that since I'd been in 1884, my leg muscles had strengthened, my arms were stronger, and my stress had gone way down. Other than the stress of fighting my feelings for Carter.

"Taylor," Carter whispered.

"Yes?" I hoped he would tell me he loved me. I hoped he would make some kind of move. *Something.*

"Get some sleep," he said after a long pause.

My heart sank as I rolled over, but I didn't sleep for a long time.

In the morning, he shook me awake. "Wake up, sleepy head."

"I'm up," I said, taking a moment to remember why I was sleeping in Carter's bed. I was disappointed when I remembered the reason.

I bustled around making a hearty breakfast of bacon and eggs, and when the men came in, we ate quickly, and then rushed out the door.

"Oh, Taylor!" Carter called, just as we were about to pull out of the driveway. "Wait a second! I have something to give you!"

My uncle winked at me. "Now I know why you don't want to leave."

Carter ran back into the house and returned a few moments later with an envelope. "Could you mail this for me?" He handed me the money for postage. *It was addressed to Charlotte!*

"Sure," I said, trying to force my smile to remain on my face. "No problem."

"Thanks!" he said and ran to his own wagon.

We left the driveway, our horses pulling us towards town, and Carter's pulling him in the opposite direction. To the house he was building for him and Charlotte.

"Why don't you tell him?" Uncle Charlie asked.

"Tell who what?" I asked in confusion.

"Why don't you tell Carter you're in love with him?"

Chapter 20

So, it was obvious. Annie could see it. Uncle Charlie could see it. How come Carter couldn't see it? Maybe he *could* but he just chose not to act on it. How many times had we come so close to kissing, but he pulled away? Like Daniel, it was clear that nothing was ever going to materialize with Carter.

While we rode to town, and Uncle Charlie went on and on about his inventions, my mind wandered over my options. *Could I actually handle going back to my life in the future? Even with a divorce, would I ever really be happy? Of course, I wouldn't have to work as hard. Or would I?*

I was still young. Just 32. Surely I would be married again at some point in my life. The question is, what kind of man did I want? In the 21st century, it seemed frighteningly easy for a spouse to cheat, whereas in the 19th century, people were too . . . settled. Infidelity was regarded as practically a crime, and with it came shame and shunning. The past was definitely a God-fearing place. For the most part.

Regardless of what time period I settled in, I knew I wanted to be with my children. Wherever and whenever we lived, as long as we were together, I would be okay. If Carter had someone he was already committed to, I had no right to interfere with that. I needed to get my act together and focus on what was really important. And that was getting home!

"Okay, I'll go with you," I told Uncle Charlie when we reached town. "On the trail west."

"You will?" he asked. His smile spread from ear to ear. "Great!"

He dropped me off at the post office and proceeded to the mercantile.

"Oh, you're back!" The elderly man behind the counter said. He'd never actually introduced himself, so I still had no idea what his name was. And so much time had passed that I didn't have the nerve now to ask him.

"Listen, I'm sorry, but I'm going to be heading west tomorrow," I said. "My uncle found me, and we're leaving tomorrow with a wagon train that is passing by."

"Aw," he said, looking genuinely sad that I was leaving. "It won't be the same without you."

"I'll be back though," I said. "I just don't know when. I do own a house here."

"Well, you'll always be welcome back," he said with a smile. "And I wish you a safe journey!"

"Thank you so much, for everything," I said.

I told Annie, who was also disappointed. The more I said it out loud, the more I accepted the fact that the distance between Carter and me would be a good thing. I needed time to get over my feelings for him.

That night in the loft when I told Carter that I'd be leaving in the morning with my uncle, he didn't seem surprised. "But I'll be back," I added hastily. "I own this house now, free and clear. And the cow. If you'd look after her for me while I'm gone, I'd appreciate it. In exchange I promise you free milk forever as long as I own her."

"Sure," he said, leaning up on one elbow and looking at me. "Just so you know, I'll miss you."

"I'll miss you, too," I said from the bed. *Just ask me to stay,* I begged in my mind. All he had to do was just say he wanted to be with me, and I would stay. I'd figure out how to get the device from my uncle once he'd finished it. He could mail it to me with directions!

"Tomorrow will be a long day for you," he said softly. I waited. "So, you should probably get some sleep now. Good night." He blew out the lamp, and only the moonlight streaming in allowed me to see him roll over away from me.

"Good night," I said quickly, before a heartbreaking sob that stuck in my throat could get out.

But it was not a good night. I analyzed every single word we'd exchanged since we'd met. He'd flirted. He'd proposed several times. *How could he not love me? How could I have misread everything he'd said? How could he not see how I felt?*

I stared at his silhouette until I worked up the courage to whisper, "I love you."

I waited, hoping he couldn't really fall asleep that quickly. His form froze, and I knew that he'd heard me. He didn't move at all for a second, but then he just silently breathed away. At least I'd *said* it. Regardless of whether he'd acknowledged it or not, I'd said it out loud to one person. The one person that mattered. If I was brave enough, I would try to tell him again when he couldn't deny he was awake.

We were awakened at four o'clock in the morning by my uncle calling my name at the foot of the ladder. "We have to go, Taylor! Get up!"

I pretended I hadn't heard until he called again. Finally, I got up. Carter left the loft so I could get dressed by lamplight. It was still dark out.

By the time I got downstairs, Carter was cooking bacon and eggs. Uncle Charlie was in and out of the house several times, carrying out the flimsy mattresses I'd made so we'd have a bit of a more comfortable sleep on our journey. He carried out my carpetbag of clothes and grabbed my sneakers that had been left drying on the mantle for a few days and threw them in the back of the wagon. Carter helped him carry my trunk of dresses.

"Are we forgetting anything?" Uncle Charlie asked as he quickly scoffed down his breakfast.

"Not that I can think of," I said.

"Then go use the outhouse before we leave," he ordered. "Because we won't be stopping anywhere along the way. I'll wait in the wagon."

I was embarrassed by my uncle's instructions. It wasn't like I was five and we were going on a road trip in a station wagon. He didn't have to *tell* me in front of Carter to go use the outhouse!

Carter just stood in the kitchen with his arms folded, grinning at me. "You heard your uncle," he said and chuckled.

I looked around the house, knowing that I would be back. Or at least, I *could* come back if I wanted to!

"If I can't handle the journey, I'll be on the nearest train back," I promised.

"Okay," he said with a nod, and we stood there awkwardly facing each other from opposite sides of the kitchen. "You have a safe journey, you hear?"

I nodded. When it was clear he had nothing else to say, I turned to walk out the door. Tears were already welling in my eyes.

"Come here," he said quickly.

I tried to will the tears back into my eyes, but that was not possible. I turned and tried to force a smile so that he'd know my tears weren't because he didn't love me or want me. He took several quick, long strides across the kitchen and grabbed me in his arms. He pulled me to his chest and held me so tightly. I wrapped my arms around his waist. I could feel that he loved me, but I waited for the words. They didn't come. Instead, he held me tightly for a few more minutes.

"We have to go!" My uncle shouted from the wagon loud enough for me to hear it from inside the house with the door closed.

But Carter didn't let go. He clung to me like he wouldn't let me go. I was okay with that. But all too soon, he released his grip. I looked up at him, hoping for the words that would make me stay. I could see his face was filled with torment. *Why won't he just tell me?*

Instead, he said, "go now."

So, I did.

Chapter 21

I cried all the way to town and managed to compose myself by the time we reached the wagon train that had just pulled into town. Various travelers went into town to trade livestock or refill supplies. Uncle Charlie introduced us to the wagon master, Earl B. Wagoner. *What an appropriate name,* I thought.

Kids ran and played, families cooked breakfast on small iron stoves or open fires, and after a couple of hours, everything was all packed up, and we were off.

"I was right!" I yelled as our wagon rattled along. It was still bumpy and even noisier full. Barrels and metal pots and pans banged together as the wagon swayed from side to side along the trail. "It does make a racket!"

After two days, we reached Weaver Settlement. "You know the train would've gotten us this far in an hour!" I couldn't believe how slow this journey was going to be.

"We get to relax and take in the scenery," Uncle Charlie enthused. "We can appreciate the beauty of nature!"

At night, we slept on the ground on our mattresses I'd made.

"See, isn't this fun?" Uncle Charlie asked, amazed at the night sky.

"As long as a wolf doesn't get us," I said. "Or a

bear."

"Not with the wagons all chained up around us," he said. "They won't get through that."

I trusted that he'd done his research and was right. I had no choice but to trust what he said. I couldn't look it up online. All of the wagons were put in a circle, and the wheels were connected by chains to the wheels in front of them. The horses and oxen were safely inside the circle to prevent them from wandering off. With small steel stoves and belongings moved out of the way, children slept inside the wagons, and most of the adults slept on the ground. Some had tents. Uncle Charlie had a tent, but he didn't want to use it, insisting we'd save it for if it rained.

Some days were chilly, and some days were hot. It was April and the weather wasn't predictable. The days and routines just flowed into each other, and I lost track of time and days and had no idea where we were. We just followed Earl B. Wagoner because he'd done this trail a hundred times he claimed. Once I did the math, I didn't believe him. If it took six months to reach California and he'd done it a hundred times, that would mean he'd been doing it for fifty years! He didn't look older than fifty, so either he was lying, or he'd started trekking back and forth across the country when he was a baby.

While my uncle went on and on about how mesmerized he was by the billions of stars in our galaxy, I thought about Carter. He seemed so far away and long ago. Like Neil. The only thing that never faded was my love for the kids.

Gradually the weather warmed into May, and we didn't have as much rain to deal with.

154

Many women walked alongside the wagons, while older kids periodically rode or walked. I didn't get to really talk to any of the other women until the supper breaks in the evening, or in the morning over breakfast before we started out. I was confined to driving our wagon while Uncle Charlie worked in the back on his zapper.

Our wagon train slowly began to turn into a bit of a soap opera. Mabel Murphy didn't like how Nelly Fry had criticized her children, either some or all of the eight she was dragging west. Olive Westby tried to lure Paul Godsey away from his bride-to-be, but in the end, Paul and Laura Harper were wed on a supper break by a Baptist minister. Olive found herself another man and the following week, a Presbyterian minister married her off to a Percy Peel on the scenic banks of a river.

"I feel like I should be writing this all down," I said after I'd filled Uncle Charlie in on the latest gossip. "Maybe if you do end up inventing Hollywood, I can invent soap operas."

We laughed, but then his smile slowly faded. "I have to tell you something," he said.

"Yes?" I asked, handing him a plate of beans and sitting beside him on a log.

"I got the Back Zapper finished," he said and let out a long sigh. "But the only way to know if it works for sure is to test it, and I don't see how we can do that."

"I'll test it," I said.

"You don't understand, Taylor," he said. "I know what I've *programmed* it to do, but I don't know that I've made any errors until we try it. We'll have to wait until we get to California to try it because I'm not going to let you be a guinea pig, and I'm not going to abandon you on this trail."

"I'll try it," I insisted. "How does it work?"

"Okay, well you are *not* going to try it," he repeated. "Because you could end up in the stone ages or in the 33rd century, *or* you could end up back to where you originally left from, if it works like it's supposed to."

"Well, we could try it together," I suggested.

"No," he said. "We'd be abandoning our horses and wagon. People would think we were kidnapped or killed by wolves, and they would just take all our stuff and move on. They would not wait for us, and when we got back, *if* we got back, we would have to make this long journey alone. That's not safe."

"So, I have to go all the way to California, and then you'll abandon me there?"

"It's a better situation," he said. "It's trial and error, but at least you won't be left out in the middle of nowhere alone."

"Okay, well, at least tell me how it works," I insisted.

"Okay," he said with a mixture of impatience and pride. "See, I used this key fob casing, and added this LED screen here that shows 140. That is the last time distance I traveled to get here. It works like a "last" button on a TV remote. When you press the button on the left, it takes you right back to the spot in space where you left. But because it warps time, and not space, as I said, time will pass continually. So, if I were to press this button, it would transport me back to my basement, but it would transport me back to the present moment based on how many days I've been gone. So, I left in April, and this would take me back to this date, May 14th, but 140

156

years in the future. All it does is reverse the number of years traveled, not the days."

"Okay," I said. "So, let's say it works, and I press the left button," I said. "Then I would arrive in your basement in May in 2024, right?"

"Right," he said. "And how many days in the future you stay before coming back, that is how many days will pass *here* before you come back. But you will come back to this very spot."

"Okay," I said with a nod. "Can I try it?"

"But, Taylor," he said. "If you were to spend one day there, when you got back here, the wagon train would be gone. You'd be alone."

"I want to try it," I begged. "Please, I miss my kids. How about if I go at night and get back before morning?"

"You are *not* going to go to Neil's house and take the kids in the night," he said, looking at me like my head was falling off.

"You mean *my* house," I said. "It's as much my house as Neil's. I pay the mortgage too."

He let out a long sigh and just looked up at the stars.

"What?" I asked. "What's wrong?"

"Well, I didn't want to tell you because I didn't want to upset you," he began. I felt my hair stand on end. He sighed again, making the wait unbearable. "The day after I saw you in the parking lot, Neil called. He asked if I'd seen you, and I told him yes. I figured out what happened when your car was left in my driveway and my time machine was flashing 140. So, I couldn't exactly tell him his wife got zapped back in time, so I said you were staying with me for a few days. I was hoping I could figure out how to build the Back Zapper by then, and your absence would only be a few days."

I nodded. "Was he worried? What did he say?" I was annoyed at myself for even caring.

Uncle Charlie sighed again and shoveled beans into his mouth to stall for time. I knew what he was doing.

"I don't know if he was worried," he said slowly. "But he brought over suitcases of your stuff a few days later and said he got the divorce papers from your lawyer."

"Good," I said. "I wish you'd told me that. I've been thinking I would have to go back and make sure he got served."

"Well, I'm telling you all this now because there's more," he said, squirming on the log and hurrying through the last of his beans. "But don't be mad."

I was instantly worried. Nothing good came after a warning not to be mad. "What?" I demanded.

"I did the best I could," he hedged.

"What?" I demanded louder. Several women seated not too far away looked in my direction.

"Well, the day I came back here looking for you was when the papers for the court hearing came for you," he said. "I guess Neil changed your mailing address to my house because I was getting mail for you then."

"What hearing?" I asked.

"A custody hearing," he said. "And this is the part where I warned you not to get mad."

"What?" I was already fuming.

"The court date is tomorrow," he said. "I opened

your mail. Apparently he is suing you to take the kids because he can't afford the mortgage and daycare now that he's a single parent. He wants you to take full custody of Emily, and he only wants the older kids on the weekdays because they'll be in school, and then they'll only have to put up with . . .."

"With what?" I asked.

"Okay, here's the other part I didn't tell you because I thought it would upset you," he said, leaning back from me a little bit when he spoke. "Around the time he brought all your stuff over to my house, he moved in another woman."

It took me a few moments to process the information. I'd known about the other woman, so I was barely surprised at Neil's behavior. He was behaving exactly as he had all during our marriage, only now with the freedom to be a public idiot. I tried to weed out the important bits of information. "So, he *wants* me to take the kids. Well, that's good."

"Well, just on weekends," he said. "Emily full time."

"Okay, well that might be best," I said. "I suppose putting August and Amber into a one-room schoolhouse where they already know the future from their history classes at school could be a problem. That will probably be fine."

He shoveled more beans into his mouth. Either he was really hungry or stalling again.

"Is there anything else you're not telling me?" I pushed. "If you've left anything out at all, I want to know right now. I don't want to be surprised."

He shook his head vigorously. "No, that's it," he

said. "I promise."

"Well, then," I said, closing my hand around the Back Zapper. "I *have* to go back now. I cannot miss a custody hearing tomorrow. I will not have my kids thinking I just abandoned them."

"Okay," he said, crossing his fingers on both hands. "Let's hope it works the way it should."

"I'm going now," I said. "I need time to prepare."

"Okay," he said. It was clear he'd given up on trying to deter me. "If anyone asks, I'll just say you're sleeping in the wagon because you're not feeling well. They'll understand why we stay behind in the morning. If you can get back right after the court hearing, we'll only be a few hours behind the wagons, and we'll catch up to them by the time they stop."

"Thanks, Uncle Charlie," I said. "For everything." I gave him a hug and a kiss on the cheek. If this zapper didn't work, I might never see him again. But I *had* to take the chance if it meant getting my kids.

I crawled up into the wagon and slipped into my jeans and T-shirt. I pulled on my sneakers that were stiff and uncomfortable from being ruined by the mud.

My heart raced as I picked up my purse and the zapper. *What if it didn't work?* Too much was at stake for that to deter me, and I squeezed my eyes shut and pressed the button.

Chapter 22

The loud buzzing in my ears cleared, and I opened my eyes. "Oh, thank God!" I yelled. I was back in Uncle Charlie's basement. I hurried out of the circle and ran up the steps to his spare room. Sure enough, the bed was piled high with my stuff. Boxes and suitcases were jumbled together with jackets just draped over the tops of them. A box on the floor was filled with sneakers, slippers, and boots, with random smaller items just thrown in. My heart instantly broke for my kids who might've had to witness Neil's packing process.

I quickly rummaged through all my things, searching for a nice dress for court. Everything was wrinkled and had just been randomly thrown into suitcases. Either Neil's girlfriend packed, or he was in a mad rush to get my stuff out in order to move her stuff in. I found my makeup bag thrown in the bottom of my shoe box.

I noticed the pile of mail on the dresser. I inspected the big brown envelopes first. I carefully read what Neil's custody wants were because Uncle Charlie has been known to get details very wrong at times. Most times, actually. But in this instance, he was correct. The custody terms said that I get the two older kids on weekends, holidays and summer vacations, and I have Emily fulltime, but he can visit her any time based on our mutually agreed-upon arrangements. I was okay with that.

As long as Uncle Charlie's Back Zapper worked, I had no problem bringing the kids back and forth.

I was too excited about seeing my kids again to sleep until an hour before my alarm on my phone went off. I had to be at the courthouse by ten.

My hair had grown, and just having a regular shower with actual shampoo and conditioner felt like a miracle. I scrubbed off the prairie dust and for the first time in months, I felt really clean. I settled on the most unwrinkled skirt and suit jacket and decided to leave my hair down. It felt so freeing after having it up in a bun most of the time to keep it out of the way. I wore heels and makeup, a luxury I'd been deprived of in 1884. I looked at myself in the mirror and hardly recognized myself. I was slim and tanned and looked and felt healthier than I ever had. It almost felt inappropriate to wear a skirt that was only knee-length!

Because we both agreed so easily on the custody terms, court was nothing more than a formality, and we were out.

I thanked my lawyer for her swift action and left the court room confidently.

"Hey!" Neil called, rushing past the lawyers to catch me before I reached the elevator. "Can we talk for a minute?"

"Sure," I said.

"You know the custody takes effect today, right?" he asked, looking worried that I had somehow failed to understand.

"I know," I said.

"So, you're taking Emily today, right?" he asked.

"Yes," I said. "I can get her now from daycare."

"Oh, she's not at daycare," he said. "I had to take her out."

"Why?" I asked.

"I forgot to pick her up just once and that witch at the daycare said they were kicking her out," he said. "That is the worst daycare! I was thinking I should sue them."

I just shrugged. "So, she's at home?"

"Yes," he said. "You can pick her up now."

"Okay," I said. "Thanks." I turned and pressed the elevator button.

"You can hang around and wait for Amber and August to get home if you want," he offered. "They haven't seen you in a while."

I was surprised he wasn't more accusatory about me being gone. I'd expected he would've tried to say I'd abandoned my children, and he wanted full custody, but instead, Neil being Neil, all he wanted was a break from being responsible for someone other than himself.

"Okay," I said. "When they get home, just bring them over to Uncle Charlie's."

"Okay," he said. "Um, listen, it's close to lunch."

"Oh, it is!" I said. "Wow, it didn't seem like we were in there that long!"

The elevator doors opened, and I stepped in.

"I was thinking," Neil said quickly, running into the elevator behind me. "If you have time, we could get a coffee, or lunch or something before you pick up Emily."

"Well, I do have some other errands to run," I said, enjoying the way Neil was practically begging to spend time with me.

"You still have to eat," he pointed out. "It's not

like a date or anything, you know." He laughed as if that would be a ridiculous thing.

"Oh, I know," I said. "Especially since you have a girlfriend. You wouldn't want to cheat on her."

His face fell. "I just think, since you haven't seen the kids for a while, I could catch you up on them so that you won't feel like you missed out on that much," he said.

I shrugged. "To be honest, Neil," I said. "I really just want to pick up Emily. The kids can tell me how they've been themselves. I'll take Emily out to lunch."

"Oh, okay," he said. I could tell he felt awkward. If he thought for one second that I would rather spend time with him than my three-year-old, he was wrong! "I already packed all her clothes and a few toys."

"Thanks," I said, exiting the building and walking towards my car. For some reason, he continued to follow me.

"Oh wait, did you get a new phone number?" he asked. "I've been trying to call you but there's been no answer."

"Nope," I said. I got into my car and shut the door. I left him standing in the parking lot while I headed to *his* house.

However, when I arrived at his house, Emily was having a nap, and Neil's new girlfriend, a buxom redhead, insisted it was best not to wake her. I agreed since I knew Emily would have a long journey ahead. The last thing I wanted was an overtired and cranky preschooler stuck in a wagon all day. I found it a bit odd that Neil's girlfriend seemed to have more trouble letting me take my child than Neil had.

Neil rushed into the house behind me and halted with a shocked expression. "When did the sitter leave?"

"I just got home a little while ago," his girlfriend said. He made no move to introduce her to me.

"Okay, Neil, how about you just bring the kids over to Uncle Charlie's when the kids get out of school," I suggested. "I'll go run my errands now, and you may as well bring Emily over then."

"Okay," he quickly agreed.

I left as fast as I could. To see another woman in *my* home—my *former* home—made me feel things I didn't want to feel. Like I wasn't enough. I wasn't good enough. That he'd chosen *her* over me. All the confidence that I'd felt looking at myself in the mirror that morning vanished as I drove out of his driveway and headed to the mall. I tried to focus on the things I had to buy for the trip back.

I stocked up on can openers, soap, dish detergent, laundry detergent, shampoo, tampons, bags of dried fruit, a broom and a mop, and some coloring books and crayons for Emily. I stocked up on thread and needles, dry cereals, pancake mix, and a rag doll for Emily. It was small and cute, yet not made of anything that the locals in 1884 would find suspicious. Other than the tag that I could remove. I also bought Emily some cute little summer dresses that were slightly too big for her. The hem would fall below her knees and she wouldn't stand out as strange. I figured some cute little Maryjane's wouldn't be too out of place in the past. I didn't know when they began to be in fashion, but I had a feeling that we would be the family that would start trends.

I also found a rechargeable USB-powered hand-held sewing machine. That would make things easier. I tried to think what else I could get for the little house. I found some cute little cowboy boots that would just fit Emily.

For fun to show Carter, I bought a newspaper. He would be amazed at what was going on in the world today.

Once I loaded everything into my car, I realized that I still needed to eat, so I went to the food court in the mall. Fast food had never tasted so . . . bland! I couldn't believe the lack of flavor it had after having eaten home-cooked meals using unprocessed ingredients for several months.

I took all the stuff back to Uncle Charlie's house and sorted it all out, fitting as much as I could into one suitcase. I threw in every pair of underwear I owned, some slippers, some pajamas, and a couple rolls of toilet paper. If I was going to be going back and forth to pick up the kids and bring them back, I could stock up on stuff on every trip. I would leave the things specifically for the house here and get them later on, once I'd returned to Harper Falls.

When I was satisfied with everything I'd managed to cram into the suitcase, I heard a loud knock at the door. It was too early for Neil to bring the kids. No one else knew I was there!

I was surprised to find Neil on the doorstep minus the kids. I didn't say a word but just looked at him in surprise.

"Listen, Tay, can we talk?" he asked. His forehead was wrinkled, and he looked like a desperate man.

I shrugged and held the door open wider for him

to come in. "I thought we did," I said.

"I just really need to clear the air," he said. "To have closure." Of course! He needed something from me so that he didn't have to feel guilty about cheating on me.

"I accept your apology," I said.

"What?" He looked genuinely shocked.

"If you're going to apologize, I accept your apology," I repeated.

"Yeah," he said. "I just want you to know how much I regret being such an ass."

I had nothing to contribute to that comment, so I waited for him to continue.

"When I saw you today," he said, looking mournful. "I mean, I'd forgotten how beautiful you are. You're really a beautiful woman, you know that?"

"Yes," I said. He stalled at my unexpected responses.

"Well, I just want you to know that I regret my actions," he said. "And if there's ever a way I can make it up to you, if I can somehow win you back, I will prove to you that I will live every day of my life to only make you happy."

"There's not," I said. Being a pioneer had made me tough. Strong.

"I heard you quit your job," he said.

"I have a new life," I said.

"Are you with anybody?" His tone sounded like he really didn't want to know the answer.

"Not yet," I said. "But that's not a priority right now."

"Well, how do I get in touch with you if I want to visit Emily?" He changed tactics. "You never answer my calls. Do you have me blocked?"

"You can arrange it with me when I pick up or drop off the older kids," I said.

"But it says I can see her anytime I want," he said. "At a mutually agreed upon time. How are we supposed to agree on a time if I can't reach you?"

"We can agree on a time when I pick up or drop off the older kids," I said.

"But shouldn't I at least have your new number to talk to the kids if I want to?" he asked, sounding like he was going to get hostile.

"You can talk to them when you see them," I said. "My phone doesn't get a signal most of the time."

"Oh," was all he said.

"Now, it's time to get the kids from school, if you want to bring them over so I can see them for a few minutes, I would like that."

"Okay," he said. "I'll be back in a little bit."

I'd spent so many weeks worrying about encountering Neil. Worried I would become a crying mess and be torn between returning to 1884 or giving him another chance. I was relieved to find that I no longer had an ounce of love for him. I was free!

Chapter 23

I'd expected Amber and August to be angry at me for abandoning them, but instead, they rushed right into my arms. "We missed you so much!" Amber said. "Where did you go?"

Even August hugged me. I kissed them both and told them how much I'd missed them.

"Mommy!" Emily shrieked as soon as Neil carried her inside. She started crying, and I held her as tightly as I could.

"It's okay," I said. "Mommy's back. I missed you guys so much!" Tears sprang to my eyes and all four of us just hugged and cried.

"Are you taking us with you?" Emily asked.

"Do you want to go with me?" I asked her.

"Yes!" she shouted.

"Dad says we have school here, so we can go with you on weekends and holidays and for the summers," August said.

"Are you guys okay with that?" I asked.

"If we lived with you full time, would we be able to go to the same school?" Amber asked.

I shook my head no. "Unfortunately, no, sorry."

"Then, I want to stay with Dad," she said. "No offense, Mom, but it has taken me years to get popular. I don't want to start over in a new school."

"I completely understand and agree with you," I told her.

"You do?" she asked in surprise. "I thought you'd be mad."

"Not at all, honey," I told her. "I love you, and I've missed you all more than you can imagine, but I also have to do what is the best thing for you. I agree that it wouldn't be a good idea to force you to switch schools."

"I'm glad you're back," August said, still hugging me.

"Me too, sweetie," I said, kissing his head. "I've thought about you guys every single day and night while I was away."

"Where did you go?" Amber asked. "Hawaii?"

I shook my head.

"But you're all tanned," she said. "You look different."

"I spend a lot of time outside," I said.

"Are you homeless?" August asked, wide-eyed and fearful.

"No, not at all," I said. "I've been traveling with Uncle Charlie for the past month or so. It has been good for me."

We visited as long as we could, but then I realized how far behind I was putting Uncle Charlie. "I'll pick you guys up on Friday," I said.

"Oh, can we wait until school's out?" Amber whined. "I have sleepovers, and I'm on the social committee at school. Can I just start visiting when school is out?"

"Sure," I said. "Whatever works."

"I was supposed to have a sleepover this weekend," August looked at me. "Me and my friends were gonna have championships in our games."

"It's okay," I said, running my fingers through his thick hair. "How about I just pick you up when school is out for the summer, then?"

"Thanks, Mom," Amber said and hugged me. "School gets out on June 20th, but can you pick us up on the 21st?"

"Okay," I said.

"Or I can drop them off here at five, to save you a trip to the house," Neil said. It was so unlike him to be so cooperative. I had a feeling it had more to do with him wanting to keep me and his redhead apart.

After final hugs and kisses, Neil gave me a soulful look and left with Amber and August.

"Now, let's see what you brought with you," I said, checking Emily's backpack. She had a few changes of clothes, bunches of underwear, a teddy bear, and a sweater. In a suitcase, she had a raincoat, rain boots, more clothes, and a few toys. I took what clothes would be suitable for her in 1884, her toys, and raincoat and rain boots, and squeezed them all into her backpack.

Eventually, I would have to find out how Uncle Charlie had accumulated all his historic coins and do the same, but right now, I didn't have the luxury of time, even *with* a time machine. I didn't have time to order stuff online and wait around for days to have it delivered.

While Emily ate a sandwich, I bought eBooks on every topic imaginable, including history books of the late 1800s and 1900s. I bought every kind of how-to book I thought I might need. Then I changed into clean jeans and a clean T-shirt, pulling on a white blouse over it. Fashionable or not, it was too hot to wear long sleeves in the summer, and once I was back in my own house, no one but my family would see me.

When we'd both taken advantage of the luxury of a modern bathroom, I carried all of the things I'd bought for the journey down to the basement and set the ones I was taking inside the circle. I knew I couldn't use the panel to go back because that would just dump me where it had the first time. I had to use the Back Zapper to get back to Uncle Charlie. But I used the circle on the floor as a guide to how much stuff I could bring. There would be no room in the wagon to fit all those things that couldn't be used immediately. The toiletries, my suitcase of clothes for Emily and me, and threads and needles were all I would take this time, plus a few snacks.

"Okay, Emily, are you ready to go on an adventure?" I asked, grabbing my purse.

"Where are we going, Mommy?" she asked, taking my hand.

"We're going to see some animals, and Uncle Charlie," I told her. "And lots and lots of horses."

"Yay!" she said, jumping up and down. "When?"

"Now, honey," I told her, stepping inside the circle. I picked her up; just in case I couldn't take anything I wasn't holding. I didn't care if a suitcase got left behind, but I would be mortified if I lost Emily!

"Now, close your eyes," I told her.

When she'd followed my instructions, I pressed the zapper. The room filled with white light and the loud buzzing filled my ears.

Chapter 24

We landed on the ground about six feet from the wagon. Emily was crying and holding her ears. "Oh no!" I said, hugging her. "Are you okay? We just traveled through time, honey. You'll be okay."

I hugged her until she stopped crying. "Oh, you're back!" Uncle Charlie yelled, hurrying to us.

I got my bearings and looked around. There were three other wagons left besides ours. "What's going on?"

"Helen Murphy had her baby this morning," he explained pointing to the far wagon. "And Doctor Brown and Reverend Peterson stayed behind to help, and if necessary officiate at a burial."

"Is she okay?" I asked. "Is the baby okay?"

"Both are doing well," he said with a proud nod of his head. "I had a fight with the doctor because I forced him to wash his hands before he delivered the baby!"

"A physical fight?" I asked. My uncle was a short, semi-balding man that was delusionally optimistic. I had gotten a glimpse of Doctor Brown, and he was a sturdy man about my age.

"Oh yes!" Uncle Charlie insisted. "I pulled at his shirt and accidentally fell down, and he had to turn and see if I was okay. I told him I would sue him for assaulting me if he did not wash his hands. He said he didn't see the harm in it, so he washed his hands with soap and water."

I was a little impressed. Not at my uncle's fighting skills but at his determination to protect a mother and newborn. "Good for you!" I said proudly.

"Why hello there, little Emily!" Uncle Charlie said. "I haven't seen you for ages! My, you've grown!"

"Uncle Charlie!" she said, delighted to see him. "Horses!"

She was amazed to see real-life horses up close. "Can I play with them?" she asked.

"No, sweetie," I told her. "But you can pet them." I carried her over and let her pet one.

"So, are you ready to go?" Uncle Charlie asked. "We're already almost a day behind the wagon train. Thankfully, the horses can walk faster than oxen so it should only take us a few hours to catch up."

"And thankfully, all the wagons left behind are pulled by horses," I agreed.

"Thankfully!" he said with a broad grin. "Come on, let's get packed up. Everyone else is packing up."

We loaded our bags into the wagon, and I sat in the very back so Emily could watch the horses behind us. We ate packaged subs from the future for supper. When the sun began to set, despite her excitement, she dozed off on the folded wool mattress I'd made, so I made my way to the front of the wagon in the narrow aisle. I was still wearing jeans, which made it possible for me to climb over the front seat and sit beside my uncle.

"Would you look at the stars! And it's not even dark yet!" he exclaimed. "I will never grow tired of this! You know, I don't really care if I ever go back to the future! I'd be happy here for the rest of my life."

174

"Happiness is important," I said. "And I know what you mean. Life is a lot harder in some ways, but it is more real. You can really experience life here. I feel healthier than I've ever felt!"

I told him what I'd bought in the future for my house. I told him about the custody arrangements and how I wanted to be back home in Harper Falls by the middle of June.

"Somewhere around there we should be reaching River Settlement, I think," he said. "If I remember the map correctly."

"I'll look at it tomorrow," I said. It was a printed map he'd brought from the future.

We talked and watched the stars as the horse plodded along until it was too dark to continue. We resumed the journey at first light and when the sun was high in the sky, my uncle looked worried.

"What's wrong?" I asked him.

"Well, I wouldn't say anything's wrong *per se,*" he said slowly. "But according to my calculations, we should've caught up with the rest of the wagon train by now. They only go as fast as the slowest oxen, and horses are faster, so we should at least be seeing them on the horizon by now."

I looked around and saw absolutely nothing but open prairie. "I also haven't heard a train whistle this morning either." Twice a day at random times we could hear a train whistle in the far distance. "Maybe we're not going the right way!" My uncle had as poor a sense of direction as I did. He'd obviously moved the wagon since I'd been gone and for all I knew, he got it turned around. Panic hit me as I realized we possibly just led three other wagons in the wrong direction. *But what were the odds of every person in our small party having a poor sense of direction? Surely the doctor or the reverend knew which direction to go.*

"No, not wrong direction," he said. "The sun rose behind us, so that's East."

"Well, technically, the sun was to our right for a while," I pointed out. "Did we go off the trail?"

"No, I stuck to the trail," he said. "Look! Trail ahead! Trail behind! No other options."

"Well, maybe they just moved faster," I said. "Or we're all out of sync because we only put in a couple hours last night and started fresh this morning. They may just be further ahead than you realized. We should keep going."

He nodded and we continued. We stopped momentarily so he could ask the other drivers if they wanted to stop for lunch or keep going until we caught up. I fed Emily some dried fruit and dry cereal for breakfast. I appreciated the packs of wet wipes I included that helped clean and sanitize. I didn't have any garbage to throw them into, and I certainly wasn't throwing garbage alongside the trail, so I stored all of the used wet wipes in a bucket, but realized it was much easier to just use a wet cloth and hang it on a small rope that hung across the back of the wagon to dry.

Small things like garbage issues and bathroom issues made me almost decide to just leave the past in the dust, but I knew that once I got back to my little house, I would be able to create a more modern and comfortable home.

We stopped for lunch, and Emily and I picked a

few berries alongside the trail with Mrs. Brown and her boys, and Reverend Peterson's teenage daughter.

We chatted about the journey, the Murphy baby, Uncle Charlie's "fight" with Doctor Brown, and how much the Peterson girl did *not* want to go west and how her parents were ruining her life. *Some things never change,* I thought.

The stop was brief but refreshing, and soon we were on our way again. When we still didn't catch up to the wagon train by nightfall, Uncle Charlie wasn't the only one worried.

"There's something wrong," Reverend Peterson said as we all sat around a communal fire, eating salted pork and beans. "Are you sure you're leading us the right way, Charlie?"

"I'm following the trail," Uncle Charlie insisted. "You can see it as well as I can, but you're more than welcome to lead if you want. I don't mind bringing up the rear!"

"Okay, I will," the reverend said. I watched his daughter roll her eyes.

"We should've been caught up to them this morning," Doctor Brown reiterated.

I could hear disgruntled mumbles from the other wagons well into the night. I lay awake beside Emily in the back of the wagon while Uncle Charlie and the other men sprawled out beneath the stars and conversed in muted tones that I couldn't quite make out. They all sounded worried though.

At first light, we had a quick breakfast and then set off down the trail again with the sun rising into the sky behind us. "We're definitely going west," Uncle Charlie pointed out as we trailed behind the Murphys, who were behind the Browns, and the Peterson wagon led the way.

"When are we going home, Mommy?" Emily asked me as we bumped along the rocky path.

"We will have a new home, honey," I told her. "We're going on a long, long wagon ride. Then we will go on a train ride. Then we will go for a short buggy ride, and we will be at our new house."

"Okay," she said agreeably. I was glad I didn't have to make this journey with Amber. She would've complained the entire way. I was hoping that by the time she and August arrived, she wouldn't be as miserable if we were settled in a reasonably accommodating house. In the back of my mind, I was preparing myself for the emotional issues I would have with her. I thought maybe August would adjust reasonably well, but I didn't have high hopes for Amber. Hopefully, I'd be able to get her to at least be tolerable for the summer. I did worry, however, that once she'd time-traveled, she would be broadcasting it to everyone. She would probably be ridiculed for either lying or being delusional. Or worse—news of the time machine would travel, and people would break into Uncle Charlie's house and use the time machine!

I was roused from my hypothetical dilemmas by a distant train whistle. *Whew!*

"Uh oh," Uncle Charlie said.

"What? It means we're on the right path," I said. "We haven't heard a train in days!"

"I know, but it's on the wrong side," he said. "We didn't cross a railroad track, so I think we're lost."

The others must've realized it too because one by one the wagons slowed to a stop, and the men got out and gathered. Uncle Charlie joined them. I started to get out, but he held up a hand. "No," he said. "This is men's business. You're not in the 21st Century anymore!"

So, I sat, dismayed at being left out, but accepting it for what it was. When the women and children got down from their wagons and stretched their legs, I got out and lifted Emily down. She immediately ran to the other children close to her age. I was pleased to see her make friends so easily. They ran and played tag. Their laughter was music to my ears. I'd dressed Emily in the cotton summer dress that came below her knees and high stockings that were normal for the period. She preferred the little cowboy boots I'd gotten for her, but it seemed the other children found them odd.

The men mumbled together in one group, and I joined the other two women. Mrs. Murphy remained in her wagon. "We're clearly lost," Mrs. Peterson said. "Oh, my gracious! Look! The natives are coming! Hide!" She ran scurrying to grab her sons and pull them into their wagon. The men hurried to grab their guns. All I saw was one lone rider far in the distance.

"Get in the wagons!" the men yelled.

I grabbed Emily and lifted her into the back of the wagon. I climbed in, and we hid down in the narrow aisle between all the barrels and baskets. I pulled a blanket over us and hoped that if it was the goods they were after, they might not notice us. If they shot at us, or used bows and arrows, we'd be safer in the middle of the wagon. But then I remembered a horrific image from some book I'd seen at some time in my childhood. *Flaming arrows and burning wagons!* Or maybe it was a movie. For some reason, that image flooded my mind.

I kept my thoughts to myself and focused on talking to God. The hoofbeats got louder and closer, but as far as I could tell it was only one. Then I heard the low mumbling of the men.

"You can come out, ladies!" Doctor Brown yelled. "It's one of our men!"

I sat up and clutched my daughter to me, thanking God that this had been a benign incident. But what if it hadn't? What if I'd selfishly brought my child from a relatively safe future to this dangerous past?

I'd foolishly imagined I could protect her from possible accidents; I'd fashioned an unsettling seatbelt of sorts from a three-layer folded cotton strip that I used to tie to the back of the wagon seat so she could ride between me and Uncle Charlie, but if the wagon were to go over a cliff, or somehow tip over, she would be hurt! On top of that, Uncle Charlie and I would go flying and my poor child would be left an orphan without even the ability to return to her father. But I'd never considered actual violent encounters that my children would have to endure.

"Hey, you okay in there?" Uncle Charlie peeked into the back of the wagon.

I nodded. Uncle Charlie reached for Emily, setting her on the ground. I crawled to the edge and swung my feet over. A hand reached out to help me.

"You okay?" a familiar voice asked. *It was Carter!*

Chapter 25

"What are you doing here?" I asked in shock, gladly taking his hand.

He gave me a lopsided grin as my feet hit the ground. "I'm heading west to pick up Charlotte," he said. "I caught up with Earl's wagon train a couple days ago. Last night, Earl was worried because you guys didn't catch up with him, so I volunteered to go back to make sure nothing happened. I found the campsite and saw you'd all moved on, so I figured since I didn't meet you on the trail, y'all must've taken the right fork in the trail when y'all should've taken the left."

"It was getting dark when we stopped for the night the other night," Uncle Charlie admitted. "I guess it was my fault. I'm sorry, folks." Mumbles of forgiveness and annoyance rumbled amongst the men.

"If we go ahead another mile, there's a brook," Carter expertly pointed out to the men. "We can let the horses rest for a bit, eat, refill water, and then start heading back. We have over a day's journey just to get back to the fork, then about another two days to catch up to the rest of the wagon train."

Everyone got back in their wagons, and we followed Carter another mile in the wrong direction before coming to the promised brook. The horses drank, we prepared a good lunch, refilled canteens and water barrels. Emily ran and laughed with the other children under the watchful eye of the Peterson's daughter, and I joined the other women in washing clothes in the brook, downstream of the drinking water. The other women hung the clothes over a rope draped from the front to the back of the wagon covers. I didn't want mine to get all dusty again, so I strung a rope from one end to the other on the inside of the wagon, a full 12 feet. The prairie wind blowing through the wagon had the clothing dried almost before we set off again towards the fork.

Emily played with the rag doll behind the front seat of the wagon, and I sat beside Uncle Charlie. Carter rode past to the front and chatted with the reverend for a while. I couldn't help but watch him. I saw him glance back at me, and I looked away. *He has Charlotte*, I reminded myself. I'd already told him I loved him, and he hadn't said it back. He'd chosen Charlotte. She was the one he wanted. I had nothing more to say. But still, I couldn't help watching him whenever I could get away with it.

Carter slowed his horse until he was beside our wagon. "Fancy meeting you here!" he said with a grin.

"Go figure!" I replied. "Oh, if you're here, then what happened to Bessie?"

"Don't worry," he said. "That's what I wanted to tell you. I left her with the Henderson's until we get back. I told them we'll give them free milk for a year."

"Oh, you'll be coming back?" I asked. I hadn't expected he would want to come back to my place. But maybe he just meant Harper Falls in general.

"Yeah, once I get Charlotte," he said.

"Oh, is your house finished?" I asked.

"It will be soon enough," he said, and pulled away, heading to the front of the line.

"You should tell him how you feel," Uncle Charlie said, nudging me in the side with his elbow.

"You heard him," I said. "He has Charlotte."

"Still, he doesn't have Charlotte *yet!*" Uncle Charlie pointed out. "It'll take another five months before we reach California, more if *I* lead the way!" He laughed. "There's time to change his mind!"

"Uncle Charlie!" I said, hoping I sounded like this was the grand finale of this argument. "I am *not* going to fight for a man! If he wanted me, he would've said so when I told him I loved him! He never said a word. He doesn't love me. He doesn't want me. Please don't say anything else about it!"

"Well, maybe if you let him know you're divorced now, he might change his mind," Uncle Charlie insisted.

"He doesn't even *know* about Neil," I told him. "I've never mentioned Neil to him, and only once when he'd seen a picture of him, I'd said I didn't want to talk about it. I never told him he was my husband."

Uncle Charlie was finally silent. He was silent for about a mile.

"Look, I'm not mad." I finally broke the silence. "It's just there is nothing you can suggest that I haven't already thought."

"Well," he said slowly, leaning away to the left.

"Uh oh," I said. "What is it you're not telling me now?"

"Well, the first night I stayed at your house, when we were out in the barn talking and taking care of the animals," he began, speaking as slowly as he possibly could to stall the inevitable bad news. "I kinda mentioned to him that you said you were anxious to get back to your husband and your children."

"What?" I yelled. "I never said that! I *never* said that!"

"When we were on the train, I think," he said. "Or no, maybe it was on the wagon ride to your house. To be honest, I don't remember exactly when it was, but somewhere on the way there, you told me you were so excited to be going home to Neil and the kids!"

"I *never* said I was excited to be going home to Neil!" I insisted. "I might've said I was excited to get back to my kids, because I was. The only way that Neil factored into my plans was in divorcing him! I'd already filed for divorce before I left! You *knew* that because you'd seen the divorce papers!"

"I know, but I thought you wanted to make up with him!" he said. "And that was before I told you about the divorce papers coming in, and the custody hearing, and Neil's new girlfriend!"

"I knew about Neil's girlfriend before I even left!" I said. "That's *why* I filed for divorce! That's why I was crying in the parking lot when you saw me!"

"Oh dear," he said. "I am so sorry, Taylor. Do you want me to talk to Carter?"

"No," I said. "No thank you! From now on, don't say anything about me to anyone, okay?"

"I'm sorry, Taylor," he repeated. "I misunderstood! I can explain it to him!"

I shook my head. This time I *was* mad. Uncle Charlie frequently got details wrong in his stories.

Sometimes it was laughable. Sometimes merely amusing. In this case, it was tragic. It was already too late for me to get Carter back. He was already on his way to get his girlfriend. She was already expecting him! That was probably what that letter was about that he'd had me mail. *Uncle Charlie's misunderstanding is why Carter sent that letter! It was immediately after!* This realization made me even angrier! *No wonder Carter hadn't said a word when I told him I loved him! He must think I'm some cheating woman! In 1884, that's practically against the law, and definitely against societal acceptance! He probably doesn't want to touch me with a ten-foot pole!* My thoughts raced violently through my head. If Carter really thought that about me, then I was surprised he would even speak to me at all. I was so ashamed. Ashamed for what Carter *thought* I'd done! How would he possibly want a woman that is disloyal?

I was so angry, I couldn't bear to sit beside my uncle for one more second, so I carefully stood up to crawl over the seat and into the back to sit with Charlotte.

"Sit down," Uncle Charlie said. "It's dangerous!"

"I've done it before," I said. Although, that had been from the back to the front, which was considerably easier. And I'd been wearing jeans at the time. Now I was wearing a long dress, uncomfortable shoes, and I still hadn't properly hemmed my dresses. Mainly because I hadn't wanted people to see my sneakers, but now that I mostly wore the contemporary shoes of the day, I still hadn't gotten around to hemming the dresses.

As the wagon swayed and tilted over the rocks, I lost my balance and fell from the wagon. The ground met me with a hard thud that I heard before everything

went black.

Chapter 26

"Taylor, can you hear me?" I opened my eyes to see Doctor Brown's face above mine. "Can you speak?"

"Oh, my neck hurts," I said, moving my head from side to side.

He examined my head. "Somehow you didn't seem to have hit your head. I don't feel any bumps."

"I learned how to fall in gymnastics," I mumbled. "In school."

"She still might have a concussion," Doctor Brown told Uncle Charlie. "She's babbling." Then he turned back to me and asked, "Are you able to sit up?"

I grasped his hand and noticed Carter's worried face in the group surrounding me. I sat up. My back ached, and my neck hurt.

"I'm fine," I said. "Just everything hurts, but nothing seems broken." Much to my own amazement. The wagon seat was about six feet from the ground and had been moving.

"You probably pulled some muscles," Doctor Brown mused.

"She did twist when she fell," Uncle Charlie confirmed.

I was still mad at him, but I wasn't worried about my health. In a worst-case scenario, I could use the zapper to get myself to a modern hospital. I stood up to demonstrate my wellbeing and hobbled back towards the wagon. All of the muscles in my shoulders and back hurt. "I'm fine!" I announced, and the others slowly dispersed back to their own wagons.

"Here, let me help you up," Carter offered, putting his arm around my back. "Are you sure you're okay?"

"I'm not sitting in front with *him!*" I said vehemently.

Carter looked confused.

"It seems we had a bit of a spat," Uncle Charlie explained. "Carter, would you mind riding here with her and letting me ride your horse? I would love to feel like a *real* cowboy!"

I glared at him. I knew what he was doing.

"I can ride in the back," I said.

"I don't mind," Carter said, looking at me with a raised eyebrow. "That is if you don't mind sitting beside me."

"It's settled then!" Uncle Charlie said. He had to get Carter to help him mount the horse, but I was surprised when he adeptly trotted along. Apparently, he'd been on a horse before!

Carter helped me into the wagon and then climbed up on the other side.

"You sure you're okay?" Carter asked me again. He was unshaven and tanned, but his blue eyes still sparkled. I nodded.

"Are you okay, Mommy?" Emily asked.

"Yes, I am, sweetheart," I told her.

"Hey there, sweet pea," Carter said to Emily.

"Hi," Emily said shyly and went back to playing with her doll. "Uncle Charlie told me to stay in the wagon, and I was worried, Mommy."

"Well, thank you for staying in the wagon, sweetie," I said. "Mommy is fine."

"Yes, Mommy *is,* " Carter said in low tone, looking away. He probably thought I couldn't hear him. I was not going to say a word. I'd told him once how I felt, and I wasn't going to put myself out there again.

Still, I did need to clear up one issue. "Just so you know," I whispered so Emily wouldn't hear over the rumbling of the wheels and the clanking of the supplies. "I'm *divorced.* I filed for divorce before I left 2024 because Neil, my husband, was cheating on me. Uncle Charlie told you that I was anxious to get back to Neil and the kids, but I *never* said that. I'd said I was anxious to get back to the future, to see my kids, and he'd taken that to mean that I'd wanted to see Neil too. Which I did not."

"Okay," Carter said, looking straight ahead in a thoughtful gaze. He was obviously trying to calculate if I was worth changing his plans for. "So, are you planning on settling out west, or going back to Harper Falls?"

"As soon as we reach River Settlement in about a month, I'll be catching the train and heading back to Harper Falls," I explained. "I want to get back home before my older kids come for the summer."

"I see," he said. "The train is pretty fast and would get me back from California a lot quicker."

So, he was still going to California! My confession had made no difference to him at all!

"Maybe what I'll do is sell my horse to your uncle," he said thoughtfully. "And I'll catch the train from California after I get Charlotte. Then I'll be back in

Harper Falls in a week or so after that."

"Sounds like a plan," I said coldly. It was clear that Charlotte was still his first choice.

"I'm glad you're okay," he said, smiling at me.

"Thanks," I said. At least I knew that he hadn't *not* chosen me because he didn't have all the facts. He now knew everything and *still* didn't want me.

"I missed you," he said solemnly.

I didn't know what to say. Missing someone and loving someone were two different things. I missed the internet but couldn't say I loved it. I knew I had to fill the gap with something, so I said, "Oh, I brought you something from the future."

"Oh, really?" he brightened up. "What is it?"

"It's a newspaper from the year 2024," I said.

"Really!" he exclaimed. "I can't wait to see it!"

"I also downloaded a lot of videos to a tablet so you can see how to build things of the future," I said. "And I got hundreds of books downloaded onto my phone with directions for everything from building a solar panel heater to building a septic bed."

He just nodded but didn't say anything, so I wasn't sure which parts he didn't understand.

"Sounds like you came prepared," he said at last.

We rode in silence for a while. He was likely thinking about his girlfriend. But at least it was better than riding with Uncle Charlie. I could not stand him at the moment.

When the sun was low in the sky, we stopped by a river. The men took care of the animals while the women cooked. I cooked salt pork and beans.

"Join us for supper!" Uncle Charlie said to Carter. I cringed, but Carter happily joined us.

"That's mighty kind of you," Carter said. "Charlie, I was thinking. When we reach California, would you like to buy my horse?"

"Would I?" Uncle Charlie said. "Of course I would!"

"Great," Carter said. "I'll be bringing Charlotte back east on the train."

"Oh, I see," Uncle Charlie said, clenching his jaw and looking uncomfortable. "This supper is delicious, Taylor! Carter, isn't she a good cook?"

"She's learning," Carter teased and winked at me.

"Finished, Mommy!" Emily said, handing me her empty plate. "I'm sleepy! Can you read me a story?"

"Sure, sweetie, just give me a minute to finish my supper, okay?" I said. I quickly ate the last of my food and set my plate down beside Uncle Charlie. "I believe you said you're doing the dishes tonight, Uncle."

He looked surprised but nodded. "Of course," he said. It was going to take more than just doing dishes to get back on my good side, but it was a start.

Chapter 27

After Emily was sound asleep in the aisle of the wagon, I tried to sleep, but I couldn't. I was exhausted and ached everywhere, but I was also still angry at Uncle Charlie. If he'd never told Carter something that wasn't true, then he never would've written back to Charlotte, and everything would've worked out. Now I didn't have anyone in either century, except for kids in both.

From where I lay across the end of the wagon, I could see the stars. Life was just so different here. In a good way. But also, in a hard way. *Is this really the best choice for me and my family?* I wondered. The whole reason I'd gotten here anyway was by accident. If I hadn't accidentally zapped myself back in time, none of this would've ever happened. I would've divorced Neil, moved on with my life and eventually met someone else. I would not have fallen for a person that had lived his whole life and died before I'd even been born.

I realized that Uncle Charlie and I had already changed history. By Uncle Charlie waiting for me, he'd caused three other families to get lost on the trail west and end up losing several days of travel. What if one of them had died because of us? That thought sent chills down my spine. I didn't want to be responsible for changing history.

I thought back and wondered how many lives I'd

already affected. Who would've taken the post office job if I hadn't filled in for Irene? Who would've taken my hotel room if I hadn't been here? Each person that I'd spoken with since my arrival had been delayed for our conversations. *What if just by being here, I've somehow messed up future generations!*

I vowed to myself that once I arrived back at my little house, I would spend the summer there, allow the kids to experience pioneer life, but we would keep to ourselves on our homestead. We would interact with as few people as possible. Then I would return back to my own world and deal with whatever hand I was dealt. If I'd been *meant* to be in the 19th century, I'd have been *born* in the 19th century!

Once I reached that firm resolution, I relaxed. I'd always been good when I'd had a clear plan. And now I had one. I decided to just ignore the fact that Carter even existed. It was a fine resolution that lasted five minutes until he knocked on the end of the wagon.

"Are you awake?" he whispered.

"Yes," I said and sat up, groaning at the aches in my back. "What?"

"Can we talk?" he asked. "Out here? Under the stars?"

I considered the difficulty in getting down in my nightgown. *Okay, fine, this will be the last time and then after this, Carter does not exist to me!* I nodded, pulled on my sneakers from the future and allowed him to help me down from the wagon. I grabbed my blanket to wrap around me since I hadn't thought to bring a housecoat.

We walked a little distance away while the rest of the camp slept. We only had the full moon to light our way.

I was silent. I had already said everything I'd had to say. He was the one that had said he wanted to talk so I wasn't going to say a word. I would just listen.

Suddenly he sat down on the ground and reached up his hand. "Join me?" he asked.

I put my blanket on the ground and sat on it. The prairie wind was warm. I waited, and still he said nothing.

"What did you want to talk about?" I prompted.

His head bobbled from side to side for a second before he could manage to get his words out. "Taylor," he said and then stopped. I waited. "I don't think you know how I feel about you."

I waited. I was tempted to say I didn't know because he didn't tell me, but I kept my mouth closed and waited. When I could see he was waiting for a response from me, I found one.

"Are you going to tell me?" I asked. If he said he cared for me and we'd always be friends, I decided I would smack him.

"It's just," he stumbled through his words. "I mean, how can you not *see?*"

"See what?" I asked coldly.

"Look at me," he said softly, turning towards me. He touched my chin and turned my face towards his. "I've been in love with you since the moment I laid eyes on you."

His confession shocked me. I was confused. "You never said anything," I said.

"I did!" he insisted. "Heck, I asked you outright to marry me! I hinted that I wanted you to marry me!

194

Heck, I even carried you over the threshold!"

I looked down. *Why was he telling me this now?*

"So, you *do* want to be with me?" I asked. My voice was uncertain, even to my own ears.

"Of course, I want to be with you!" he said. "Nothing made me happier than when you told me you weren't in love with Neil!"

I nodded.

He touched my chin and tilted my face up to his. "I love you, Taylor." His eyes roamed over my face, and then his fingers were brushing my cheek as he lowered his lips to mine. When he pulled away, his voice was lower and softer. "I've been wanting to do that since before you told me you were from the future. It broke my heart when you left."

He kissed me again, and his fingers wove through my hair and dissolved any ideas I'd had about ignoring his existence. Carter Richards was the man I was meant to be with. I could feel it in my bones. Somehow, it was exactly right. I could tell he was feeling the same way.

We kissed and cuddled and talked in hushed whispers until dawn lightened a line on the horizon. "You better get back to bed," he said.

We hurried across the dewy grass, and he helped me back into my wagon. I was too excited to sleep, but I couldn't erase the smile that came from knowing I was loved.

Chapter 28

The following days and weeks were filled with flowers and laughter and middle-of-the-night clandestine lovemaking in the tall prairie grass. Carter frequently rode up beside our wagon and handed me a bunch of daisies or other wildflowers. Sometimes he'd let Uncle Charlie ride his horse so he could ride with me. Sometimes I rode on Carter's horse with him. He'd even taken Emily for a horse ride every now and then.

With only two more days to go to reach River Settlement, I grew more excited about settling down in our little house. I wondered what August and Amber would think of Carter. August was sure to like hanging out with him, and Amber loved horses. I could imagine her excitement at having her own horse.

"Your turn, missy," Carter said to me as Uncle Charlie stopped the wagon. Carter hoisted Emily off the saddle in front of him and handed her over to me in the wagon. Then he reached over and helped me climb into the saddle in front of him. "We'll bring up the rear!" he shouted to Uncle Charlie.

He turned his horse around and walked it to the end of the long wagon line. "Now we have privacy," he said into my ear as we followed behind. "Now I can tell you how much I love you, and no one can hear."

"Would it be so bad if everyone heard?" I asked

with a laugh.

"Not at all," he said, and kissed my neck. "I love you with all my heart, future girl!"

I finally had found peace. The warm prairie wind blew, while the sweet smell of flowers and berries wafted on the breeze. Carter's strong arms around me made me feel secure.

"In just two days we'll be at River Settlement," I reminded him. "Then in five days, we'll be back in Harper Falls, and you'll get to meet August and Amber. I'm just worried that they might have a bit of an adjustment at first, like I did."

"Well, *you and Emily* will be back in Harper Falls," he corrected. "I won't get to meet your other kids until I get back from California."

"You're *still* going to California?" I asked in shock. "I thought you were coming back with me!"

"Well, I *have* to finish the journey to California," he said. "Charlotte is expecting me! I can't disappoint her!"

"Well, send her a letter from River Settlement," I suggested. "I'm sure she'll get over it!"

"Taylor, I can't believe you're like that," he said with all essence of love and admiration gone. "How can you be so selfish?"

"Selfish?" I said. "Because I want you all to myself?"

"You don't *have* me all to yourself!" he said. "You've got your kids!"

"Okay," I said.

"Okay?" he asked, but both of our voices had changed from light and warm to deep and cold.

"Of course," I said. "Whatever you want."

"So, I want to make sure," he said. "When Charlotte is in Harper Springs, you're not gonna be mean to her, are you?"

"I won't purposely *try* to be mean to anyone," I said. "But if she says anything to me, I'm likely gonna be mean! Do you actually expect me to like her?"

"You know, Taylor," he said, urging his horse to a fast trot and catching up to my uncle. "I was so wrong about you."

Uncle Charlie pulled over and stopped and Carter dismounted. He didn't even help me off the horse! I got off and stomped away fast enough that he couldn't see the tears already welling up in my eyes. *The nerve!* Carter rode off at full gallop to the front of the line.

I climbed up beside Uncle Charlie. "What's going on?" he asked.

"Nothing," I said. "He is a jerk. He says he loves me and wants to be with me, but he is still bringing his girlfriend to Harper Falls and expects that if I see her in town, I won't be mean to her!"

"What a jerk," Uncle Carter agreed. "Well, there's plenty more fish in the sea."

"I'm done fishing!" I said.

"What's wrong, Mommy?" Emily asked.

"Nothing, sweetheart," I said. "Mommy just isn't getting along with Carter right now, that's all."

For the following two days, Carter ignored me completely. I hardly even saw him until on the night before we reached River Settlement, I saw him laughing and eating supper with a girl that was about in her early 20s. *He's just like Neil!* I realized men in the 19th century were no better than men in the 21st century! What was even the point of remaining here?

When we reached River Settlement the following afternoon, Uncle Charlie gave me a few bundles of cash. "I can get more any time I want it," he said. "But make sure you stuff it into your mattress when you get home! It's all in ones and there are $100 in each bundle."

"That's $1000!" I whispered harshly.

"I'm rich!" he whispered enthusiastically. "I'm living my best life, and there's more where that came from!"

"But, if I have the Back Zapper with me, how will you get to the future?" I asked.

"I know where you live," he said with a laugh. "And I can afford to take the train!"

"Okay," I said. "What if it breaks?"

"Just write me a letter," he said. "I'll write to you as soon as I reach California."

"Okay, thanks for everything," I said. "I'll keep the cash for when I come back, but I think after I send a letter to the Hendersons telling them they can keep the cow forever, but just to give me free milk whenever I'm back in town, I'm just going back to the future. If it's okay with you, can I stay in your house until I get an apartment or something?"

"Sure, whatever you want," he said. "But I don't think I'll be going back to the future ever. I actually really like this kind of life. I've lived my whole life wanting adventure and never being able to have it. Now look at me! I'm a cowboy!" He tipped his new cowboy hat at me.

"I'm glad you're having fun," I said.

"Listen, Taylor," he said. "I was going to leave the house to you in my will anyway, so since I really don't plan on going back to the future ever, consider it yours!"

"Okay, thanks," I said. "Who can say no to a house with a time machine in the basement?"

"Just be careful when you touch stuff," he said. "There are other inventions that I've been working on, and I don't know for sure what will happen."

"Lesson learned!" I said.

He said goodbye to Emily, and the two of us stood on the edge of town and watched the refreshed wagons pull out. I saw Carter ride out beside the wagons. He turned his head and saw me, but he didn't wave. His expression was sad. *Let him be sad,* I thought.

Chapter 29

River Settlement turned out to be bigger than I'd expected. I left our luggage at the train station, and the guy behind the counter agreed to keep an eye on it for me. I took Emily to find a restaurant. I didn't have far to go; it was just down the street.

The restaurant was packed. "There's a table over here," a waitress said as she approached me with a tall menu.

"Wow, I didn't expect River Settlement to be so big," I said.

"Well, we have 10,000 folks here or so," she said. She pulled a stray hair back behind her ear. She was younger than I was, but she looked far more tired.

"How did it get so big?" I asked out of sheer curiosity. "It's way out in the middle of nowhere!"

"And that's how it became *somewhere*," she said with a pleasant laugh. "Some folks just stuck around after the railroad was finished in these parts, and a lot of folks stayed when they were plumb tuckered out on the trails and couldn't make it all the way to California or Oregon. And then some, believe it or not, didn't much like the life out west and turned around and came back, and this is as far as they got."

"Wow, it makes sense," I said.

"So, will you be one of the folks staying on the

way out or staying on the way back?" she asked with a pleasant smile.

"I'm leaving the trail west," I admitted. "And my plan was to leave on the first train East and go back home to Harper Falls."

"Was?" she asked and gave me a little slap with the menu as she handed it to me. "You'll be staying!"

I placed my order for Emily and me and asked about the trains.

"The train leaves tomorrow afternoon," she said. "There are three hotels in town, one's just down the street that way. One is the other way. And then one is up behind this street."

"Thanks," I said. But I wouldn't be needing any of them. Once I got a letter written and mailed, I was taking Emily back to the future.

When we had eaten our meal, and I asked about the post office, the waitress directed me down the street.

"I'm tired, Mommy," Emily said as we walked all the way down the street and finally found the post office. I picked her up and carried her the rest of the way.

Thankfully, the post office was open, and I was able to buy an envelope and a stamp. I set Emily up on the long wooden counter running alongside the wall beside a row of windows and quickly wrote a letter with one of the pens I'd brought from the future. I tore out a page from a notebook I'd stashed in my purse and wrote:

Dear Mrs. Henderson,

Thank you so much for looking after Bessie for me. I would like to give her to you as a permanent gift since I will be away for an undermined amount of time. She is free. The only thing I will ask is to buy milk from

you when I am in Harper Falls again.
Sincerely,
Taylor Cooper

It was brief, but I honestly had no idea how long a letter should be between two people who didn't even really know each other. We'd met a couple times, but mostly Carter had delivered the milk in the mornings. And he had taken the cow there.

I mailed the letter and then took Emily all the way back up the street to the train station to get our luggage.

"Where are we going, Mommy?" she asked.

"We're going home, sweetheart," I told her.

"Home to Daddy?" she asked.

"No, honey," I told her. "We're going to live in Uncle Charlie's house."

"With horses?" she asked hopefully.

"No, honey," I said. "No horses."

"You said we'd have horses," she said.

"Well, that might not work out right now," I said. "But we will have horses sometimes."

"I miss James and Tad," she whined.

"Are they from your preschool?" I asked, thinking maybe she'd be happier than I would about going back to the future.

"No, from the wagons," she said. "Will I ever see them again?"

"I'm sure you will someday," I said.

When we reached the train station, I was surprised to find that my luggage was exactly where I'd left it. It hadn't been stolen or bothered.

"Can we go on the train, Mommy?" Emily asked,

jumping up and down and clapping her hands. "Please?"

As I was about to say no, it dawned on me that if I did choose to come back to this time period in the future, I would not want to end up here so far from my little house and have to deal with three kids on a five-day train ride just to get to my own property.

"Okay," I told her, much to her delight. "In the morning!"

We stayed at the fanciest hotel in town, which was also the only one with a vacant room. There was a small dining room in the hotel, and Emily and I were treated to a luxury meal. I was beginning to see what Uncle Charlie meant about feeling rich.

In the morning, I bought our ticket and sat out on a wooden bench with our luggage and waited for the train. The platform gradually filled with other waiting travelers. I silently wondered how many of them were going east to meet their waiting husbands.

I looked up when the train whistle blew. Emily jumped off the bench and clapped her hands. "Mommy! It's a train!"

But as the train approached, I noticed something beyond it. In the distance and riding towards the train station at a furious gallop was a man on horseback. "Looks like somebody is going to miss the train," I told Emily.

Just as the train was pulling into the station and blocking my view, I recognized the rider! He was close enough to the track that I was *sure* it was Carter, and then the train rolled in between us. A symbolic sign that we were *supposed* to be apart.

"Come on, Mommy!" Emily pulled on my hand as other travelers began boarding the train. "The train's here!"

"Just a second, Emily," I said.

The train was so loud and intrusive that I couldn't hear if Carter was yelling or not. He was probably riding around the back of the train, which seemed to be quite long.

"Mommy! We have to get on!" Emily said, pulling harder on my hand.

"Just a minute, Emily," I said. "We have to take the next train tomorrow."

"Why?" she whined. "I want to go now!"

"Tomorrow, it might be a prettier train," I told her.

"Really?" she asked.

"I think so," I said.

"Is it pink?" she asked.

"I don't think so," I said. "But I think it's nicer."

"Are we going to stay in the hotel again tonight?"

"Maybe," I told her.

"Mommy, this is a really good adventure, isn't it?"

"Yes, it is," I said. I wished the people would finally get all inside. From what I could see of the length of the train, it seemed to go on for miles with cars of coal, livestock, goods, mail, and cars of people. Carter would be better off to wait until the train passed than he would be to try to go around it.

As the train finally pulled away, I was hoping Carter would still be there. I feared he may have figured I'd gotten on the train and left. But when the very last car passed, there he was; still sitting on his horse across from me with a worried look on his face.

He dismounted, tied his horse to a tree, and ran over to the platform. "Oh, thank God you're still here!" he said, grabbing me into his arms and clinging to me. "I thought you'd left!"

"I can go tomorrow," I said. "What happened? Is my uncle okay?"

"Yes, he's fine," he said, still holding me tightly. "I want to marry you! I love you!"

Tears slipped from my eyes. "So, you're through with Charlotte?" I asked.

"No," he said, and chuckled, pulling me from him to look into my eyes. "Charlotte is my seven-year-old daughter!"

I felt my face grow hot. "Oh my God," I said. "I am mortified! I thought . . . I thought . . .."

"I know what you thought," he said, with a boyish grin, pulling me back into his arms. "Your uncle told me what you thought. I've been riding since the crack of dawn to get back here, hoping to catch you."

"All those things I said about being mean to her," I said. "I had no idea she was your *daughter!* Of course, I'd never be mean to her! I'd love her as my own!"

He just chuckled. "You silly, silly girl," he said, kissing my hair. "Do you know how crazy in love with you I've been all these months?"

"No," I admitted.

"I admit, I hadn't wanted to get too involved when I found out you could possibly just zap out of my life at any moment," he said. "I tried to keep my distance when I found out you were from the future, but I couldn't help falling in love with you. Then when I heard about Neil, I figured all was lost. Then when you told me you wouldn't accept my daughter, I thought it was because you had enough kids and didn't want anymore."

"No, not at all!" I said, pulling away and looking at him. "I honestly thought she was your girlfriend! I couldn't figure out why you wanted to bring an old girlfriend back to town if you wanted to be with me!"

"Well, you are the only lady I want," he said. "I am seriously asking you this, for the last time, will you marry me?"

"Yes!" I exclaimed. "Of course, I'll marry you!"

"Alrighty then!" Carter said, kissing me with great gusto. "Come on, little lady," he said, picking up Emily. "We're going to a wedding!"

Once the manager at the train station agreed to keep our bags in the station overnight, Carter hoisted me into the saddle, and then lifted Emily up to sit in front of me. He sat behind me and wrapped his arms around me and Emily. "Hang on, family," he said. "We got us a minister to catch!"

Despite his warning, he didn't go fast, and it was sunset when we caught up with the wagon train.

"You made it!" Uncle Charlie yelled with a broad smile and open arms when we arrived. "I'm so glad it all worked out!"

By the light of campfires and stars, Reverend Peterson officiated, and Carter and I promised to love each other until death do we part. Emily clutched a bouquet of daisies which matched my own.

"I'll buy you a wedding band in town tomorrow," Carter promised me.

"Throw the bouquet!" the young girls shouted, so all the unmarried women and teenagers stood in a group behind me, and I threw my bouquet of field daises over my shoulder. I turned to see the women scrambling. Seconds later, Reverend Peterson's teenage daughter raised the flowers high in the air.

"It's me! It's me!" she shouted as if she'd won the lottery. "I'm going to be the next to get married!"

Her father didn't look too pleased, but everyone laughed. Some of the men got out their fiddles and played joyful music while the kids ran around laughing, including Emily with her new friends.

Late that night after all the children were tucked in, and the men sat and talked together and the women talked as they did dishes, Carter and I sat on the seat of my uncle's wagon and talked softly.

"Ah, there you are!" Uncle Charlie said. "I don't mean to interrupt your honeymoon, but I have a wedding present for you, but it's for tonight only. Tomorrow you have to give it back!"

"Okay," I said slowly, not sure what he could possibly give us for just one night.

"Here!" he said and handed over his tent he'd brought from the future, still in its package. "I figured you two lovebirds might like some privacy tonight. But who knows, I might need it in the future, so you may as well give it back in the morning."

"Okay, thanks," I said.

"Much obliged," Carter said, leaping down from the seat and shaking my uncle's hand. "Uncle Charlie!"

Uncle Charlie nearly burst with glee. "Welcome to the family!" he said. "You're the son I never had!"

"And you're one of my many uncles, but the only one I like!" Carter said.

208

Uncle Charlie helped us put the tent up, which was more complicated than the packaging promised. Finally, it was set up.

"There ya go, kids!" Uncle Charlie said. "Congratulations!"

"Oh, before you go," Carter said to my uncle as I crawled inside the massive tent. "Are you gonna be ready at the crack of dawn to head back to River Settlement?"

"Am I ever!" he said. "I get to be a cowboy!"

The plan was for him to ride one of his horses, I would ride one, and Carter would carry Emily on his horse with him, and we would move as fast as possible to try to catch the morning train. Carter assured me my luggage would still be fine in the morning because the train station got locked after the last train went through for the day.

So, with plans set for the future, I relaxed in the comfort of a canvas tent in the middle of a prairie, in the arms of my husband, and had never felt more loved in my life.

The end

Note from the author:

Dear Reader,

Thank you so much for taking the time to read this book. I do hope you enjoyed it.

I've always been fascinated with time-travel stories. Wouldn't it be fantastic if we could really visit any time in history? Feel free to comment on my Facebook page what your favorite time to travel to would be. I thought mine would be 1884, but after all the research, I think I'd prefer the 1980s lol.

For updates, you can find me on Facebook (www.facebook.com/ElizabethBarstone), although I am not on social media as much as I'd like to be, or visit my publisher website at www.HavenStreetPublishing.com.

Again, I appreciate that you've taken the time to read this book and make it this far.

Always,
Elizabeth Barstone

P.S. if you would like to receive an email notification when I release a new book, you can email
Elizabeth@havenstreetpublishing.com
with the subject line:
Please Add Me To Barstone Mailing List.

Other Books by Haven Street Publishing

The Porch Pirate by E. A. Hayes
The Great Snatching by Roger W. Hayes
Delaney Page & The Secret of Everything
The To Do List Solution for Adult ADD'ers.
The Aunt Solution
Benny J. & The Broken Bicycle Gang
Thurber's World

The Diary of a Teenage Mom series
1. Diary of A Teenage Mom
2. Would The Real Mr. Right Please Stand Up!
3. A Real Family
4. The Wedding Belle
5. Wedded Bliss
6. A Star is Born
7. Choices
8. Changes Happen
9. The Glass
10. A Meant-To-Be Love
11. Just One Thing

The Zoey Series:
1. Zoey Starting Over
2. Zoey Quits Again

Other Books
The Wishing Field

Diaries & Notebooks
Good Day Diary
Tough Day Diary
Five-Year Diary
101 Interviews With Friends

www.ingramcontent.com/pod-product-compliance
Lightning Source LLC
Chambersburg PA
CBHW011143310726
48972CB00009B/2823